THE MAN AHEAD

Long ago, Lara Douglas made a mistake. She took refuge afterward in Island Park, Idaho, enjoying its sleepy beauty and her proximity to family, working as a fly-fishing guide on the banks of the Snake. The rest of her days, she expected, would be without drama, passion or love. She was wrong.

The hitchhiker in front of her is Steve Mitchell, "the one who got away." The one she *sent* away. His guitar case says he's seen hard times, his lean physique and scruffy face say he's on the run, and his eyes and lips say he'll never forget what she did to him. But that voice is still sexy as hell and Lara's soul knows *now* is the time to seek forgiveness. This man once promised to make her heart and body sing, and today, no matter the danger, no matter the cost, she'll see that they finally get their chance.

YOU AGAIN

Lyn Austin

www.BOROUGHSPUBLISHINGGROUP.com

YOU AGAIN
Copyright © 2015 Lyn Austin

ISBN 978-1942886-64-8

To my parents, Jay and Rowane, who celebrate their 63rd anniversary this year. You've taught me more about true, unconditional love than anyone else. This book is also for Kerry, who introduced me to the gracefulness of fly-fishing; to David, who helped me see the romance of Island Park; for Rod, who gave me a nesting place there; and for Butch, who encourages me daily to live my dreams.

ACKNOWLEDGMENTS

To Michelle, Jill, and the gang, for making dreams come true for writers every day, and to my hardworking and honest editor, Chris Keeslar, one of the very best in the business. He knows better than anyone that without his expertise this book would be in a box collecting dust. Thank you!

Table of Contents

About the Author

YOU AGAIN

Chapter One

"All I Ask of You" from *The Phantom of the Opera* filled Lara with longing as she drove down the country road on her way to work. Softly humming the haunting melody, she headed south on the two-lane highway, the early morning light warming her left cheek. Living in Eastern Idaho had its disadvantages. A Broadway play was out of the question, as were many other cultural events, but at thirty-three years old she had chosen to give up several things she loved in exchange for the peace and contentment she felt living in the mountains of Island Park.

Lodge pole pines lined both sides of the road, and the tops of the spindly trees swayed in the persistent morning wind. Although the trees looked somewhat barren, the ground underneath was anything but dead. Thick green tufts cluttered the forest floor. Blue flax, fireweed, and blazing stars laced the land, along with a variety of other wildflowers in various pastel hues. The country lay in sections, one piece ravaged by a pine beetle invasion, the next a dense grove of emerald green pines bordering a deep river that held the same rich color as the trees surrounding it. The proud Snake wove its way throughout this valley, always flowing, even in the coldest of months, and the Henry's Fork section offered the best fly-fishing in Idaho—and many from all over the world would argue that it was the best fishing in the world.

Lara certainly felt an ease here that she had found nowhere else. After her divorce she couldn't get out of California fast enough. She'd wanted to be as far from Phillip as she could get, and Island Park was the perfect spot because its down-home friendliness and warm-hearted people were exactly the kind of "hicks from the sticks" that Phillip sneered at for their entire married life. People like her Uncle Lawrence, who had gently taken her in after that horror was finished.

Lara noticed movement ahead of her on the side of the road. Slowing considerably, she watched, fascinated, as her jeep drew nearer. More often than not she would pass an animal of some sort in the early morning. A deer, elk, moose, or possibly even a bear could easily be spotted in this valley. She never tired of seeing the wildlife, so disappointment filled her as she realized that this time the specimen was merely human.

The man turned to face her oncoming jeep and stuck a grimy thumb into the air. His grizzled face was almost completely covered with a bedraggled-looking beard, and his shoulder-length hair hung in a tangled ponytail. His faded jeans and tattered flannel shirt looked as if they hadn't been washed for a very long time, if ever. A backpack was limply strapped to his back, and he carried a guitar case covered in a fine layer of dust. His shoulders, slumped with the weight he carried, said he'd pretty much given up on life.

"Sorry, mister," Lara muttered to herself as she pressed her foot to the accelerator and sped away. "I'm not into picking up strays." A single woman would be foolish to even think about it. Many people could and did live secret lives in these mountains.

Glancing in the mirror, she watched the man fade from view. But as her reflection looked back, she noticed a worried frown cross her face. Something was vaguely familiar about that hitchhiker.

Thoughts of the man were pushed to the back of her mind as she parked the jeep in front of her uncle's fishing business. The TroutHunter was the most popular resort in the section of Island Park known as Last Chance. The combination inn, elegant dining, fishing and guide service and tackle shop provided everything a fisherman would need for staging a great adventure in the outdoors. During her childhood, Lara had spent her summer vacations here in Island Park helping her aunt and uncle around the old lodge they ran and learning everything she could about fly-fishing. Even after college and her father's untimely death she'd continued to spend as much time as possible with them, and after her divorce Uncle Lawrence invited her to come back and help him run the place permanently. Lara had gratefully accepted.

The log and rock structure, nestled on the banks of the river, was in the perfect location for fly-fishing. Right on Henry's Fork, this was the best place for a first-timer to get into his fishing gear and step into the clear, cold water. Lara had been teaching newbies the sport for years here. The river was only about knee-high, and there weren't trees close to the bank, so there was less chance of a fisherman getting his line snagged. She also knew of some great five-to-eight pound trout that enjoyed giving a tug on a novice's pole, wily fish who probably weren't too worried because they knew the rule here was catch-and-release.

A good fisherman always watched the water before picking a spot, and since her scheduled client hadn't yet arrived Lara slipped into her neoprene waders and her fly-fishing vest then walked to the water's edge to see what might be bubbling up along the surface. Two brilliant white swans glided regally past, and she watched a few trout rise into view. The caddis fly hatch was on. There were several of the moth-like creatures skimming the top of the water.

Taking a handmade fly from her vest that looked just like the bugs, Lara walked back to her jeep to get her pole. A black SUV with Nebraska plates pulled in beside her, the man who had hired her to teach him to fly-fish. Lara took a step toward him as he climbed from his vehicle, but out of the corner of her eye she noticed the hitchhiker from earlier shuffling along the side of the highway, his shoulders slumped, looking at his feet. He had walked a couple of miles at least, so her next thought was that he must be in better shape than she'd imagined.

Dismissing the stranger once more, Lara turned to her client. John Carson was a doctor from Omaha, and he had driven to Idaho for "a month's worth of an Ernest Hemingway kind of lifestyle." Lara thought that idea somewhat off, since Hemingway committed suicide in Idaho, but she wasn't about to turn down anyone who wanted to stay at The TroutHunter and pay for fishing lessons. She held out her hand to introduce herself, but as she did she noticed the hitchhiker momentarily stop to reposition his duffle bag and beat-up guitar case. A bright splash of color on the case caught her eye. Lara flipped her dark ponytail just in time to read, under a sheet of dust, the words COZUMEL '99.

She froze. *Now* she knew what had seemed so familiar. The guitar case, the Cozumel sticker… She had peeled the back from that exact sticker and placed it on that exact case fifteen years ago. But how could this possibly be Steve? Granted, the man's coloring was the same, but Steve had been a good-looking, clean-cut guy with the most exquisite green eyes she had ever seen. This hitcher couldn't possibly be the Steve Mitchell she dated in high school and college.

He didn't look in her direction. She wanted to say something—*needed* to say something—to call his name, but she couldn't find her voice. Then she realized she was still shaking her client's hand.

Quickly, she recovered enough to speak.

"Doctor, we are thrilled to have you stay with us this month. I know how anxious you are to get started on fishing. We're going to do that for the morning, and then after lunch we can take a drift boat down the river if you'd like. I've been watching the water, and the caddis fly hatch is on." She pulled another tied fly from her pocket and handed it to him. "Do you know how to tie this onto your line?"

Dr. Carson nodded and moved to show her his brand-new fishing gear, but Lara couldn't stand it any longer. She rudely interrupted.

"I'm so sorry, John, I have to run a quick errand. Can you get your gear on? I will be back in five minutes. Don't go into the water before I get back. A good fisherman always studies the water from the bank first. I'm sorry, but I really will only be a few minutes."

She rushed to the driver's side of her jeep, jumped in and started the vehicle in one swift motion, pushed the gearshift into reverse and backed out onto the highway. All the while, she felt a sense of dread and panic fill her body. Her heart began pounding. Her throat felt parched as if she'd just run a marathon. Already she was questioning her decision to go after him, and she hadn't even gotten very far. Why was she doing this?

But she knew.

What had happened to him over the years? The question whirled in her brain like the refrain of an unfairly catchy song. When she had last seen him, he had been everything a girl could want. But she had let him go.

No, that wasn't true and she knew it. A shudder slid restlessly up her frame. Steve had left because of what she'd done, and she could never blame him for her mistakes. He had treated her like a precious flower waiting to bloom, and she had treated him like…shit. There was simply no better way of putting it. She'd naively thought she could win him back after he walked out of her life, too, but she'd been wrong. He wouldn't take her calls or see her. Then one day she'd heard from a mutual friend that he'd changed colleges. She'd never seen him again.

Fifteen years was a very long time. What if he didn't remember her?

No. He would. But he might not have thought about her for years. After all, they had just been kids. Stupid, stupid kids.

A couple of years afterward, she'd run into his mother at the mall. Mrs. Mitchell had been distant and cool. Lara had asked about Steve and got an unexpectedly blunt answer: "He's okay. He'll always land on his feet, but I know that he will never get over the way you treated him and the things you did. After all you shared, all the good times you had, all the plans the two of you were making together…you owed him more than that."

That day Lara had stood in a stupor long after Mrs. Mitchell walked away. Today the same sick feeling filled the pit of her belly.

She'd thought a lot about Steve since. When their ten-year class reunion drew near, she'd even gone so far as to try and find an address for him, but his family moved and no one seemed to know where. Still, she'd vowed that someday she would apologize and let him know that he meant something special to her, even if they hadn't ended up together. And…kids did stupid things. Maybe the past wouldn't matter to him anymore.

Analyzing this could take a week, and by then he'd be long gone. One part of her mind said that was fine. Just return to the river, where all problems seemed to vanish for her. The other part told her to get it over with. Then she'd never have to see him again; her conscience would be at ease.

Didn't she want to speak with him and hear how his life had changed? From his outward appearance, it didn't look like life had been very kind to him.

"Oh, God, I don't want to do this," she said out loud to herself. "He won't want me to see him. Not in his present condition, anyway. Besides, I've got to get back to my client."

Lara's hand went to her hair, fingers twirling and twirling a long strand of her brunette ponytail. The habit had helped her solve many a dilemma in her life, though she'd tried to break the addiction after her ex-husband heaped ridicule on her for it. Of course, she couldn't remember a time since she moved to Island Park that she'd needed to twirl her hair until now.

She was stalling. If she spent the morning thinking about what to do, Steve really could be long gone. She needed to make a decision. Now.

Lara turned the jeep in the direction Steve had taken. Twirling her hair some more, she tried to get her words in order. Could she just stop and talk to him, tell him she'd been a creep and drive away? That seemed the easiest solution. Maybe it would even work.

There he was, up ahead. She held her breath as she drew nearer. Steve turned, his thumb on the way up, but when he looked at the jeep that had already sped past he put it down and started walking again.

Lara passed him then pulled over onto the soft shoulder and waited for him to catch up. Reaching over, she opened the cloth-type door. She wanted to say something normal like, "Hello, Steve," but that didn't seem appropriate. Maybe she should just skip the whole interaction. Maybe he wouldn't recognize her and she could just give him a ride and forget this mess.

His scruffy face appeared on the passenger side of the jeep, and startled green eyes peered into her hazel ones. He remembered her all right. It was written all over his face.

His eyes held her captive as if he tied her to a bed. Memories flooded her mind until her breath came in short gasps, making her breasts rise and fall against the steering wheel. They were recollections of crisp autumn days playing football in crunchy leaves, ice skating at Jones's pond on a frigid winter evening, later, snuggling in each others' arms in front of a roaring fire… So many, many memories, most of them pleasant. Steve's mother had been right. She did owe him more.

She found her voice. "Can I give you a lift?"

His expression of surprise changed to one of complete disgust. He spoke for the first time, his voice a low, raspy whisper. "You again? I might be hard up, lady, but I'm not *that* hard up."

And with that, he shifted his backpack to his other shoulder and walked away.

Chapter Two

Lara sat in her jeep in stunned silence. Whatever she'd expected, it hadn't been what she received. Heat rose to her cheeks once again as she remembered the insulting tone of his voice.

"You again?"

It had been more of a sneer than anything else.

Steve was independent as a teenager. Proud. He never could take ridicule from anybody. If someone mistreated him or showed him disrespect, he'd found it difficult to forgive them. He hadn't scorned others, and he'd expected the same esteem in return. He apparently hadn't changed. So, how was she ever going to talk to him?

Lara watched his retreating back for a few more seconds. She had always known deep inside that she'd hurt him, but until this moment she hadn't realized how much.

* * *

Steve Mitchell watched the mud-caked toes of his boots as he continued to put one foot in front of the other, wondering which part of his brain told his feet to keep walking. With everything he'd been through in the last fifteen years he would have thought nothing could possibly surprise or shock him, but he hadn't counted on this. Surely every brain cell had to be reeling from seeing Lara again.

For a split second he'd thought he must be delirious. After all, he hadn't had a decent meal for almost a month. But it only took a moment for his mind to clear, for him to realize that Lara Douglas— no, Lara…whatever, he couldn't remember what her married name was—had just offered him a ride in a shiny red jeep.

Left, right, left, right. He forced his feet to keep moving, because he had a tremendous urge to sit down under the nearest tree and bawl like a baby. She'd finally got the red automobile she'd always wanted. He'd used to lie awake nights fantasizing about buying her a red convertible for a wedding present.

He was conscious of her still behind him, sitting in the jeep with the engine running. He was relieved to finally hear the crunch of the tires in the gravel, for he knew she'd turned around and gone back the way she'd come. But where in the hell had she come from? What was she doing in the wilds of Idaho? The last time he'd had news of her, she was living in San Diego with that ass-wipe attorney she married.

She'd passed him earlier that morning. He remembered seeing the CJ-5 a second time, too, parked at an elegant lodge, but he hadn't paid much attention except for the unusual license plate that said DMSLFLY. He knew just enough about fly-fishing to know that the Idaho plate meant Damselfly, one of a trout's favorite dinners.

Suddenly it dawned on him like a piano falling on his head. Her aunt and uncle lived in this area! She'd spent many summers in Island Park helping them at their lodge, and she'd sent Steve letters filled with the wonderful adventures she'd had here. Now that he had time to think about it, she'd been wearing waders today. So she must have been fishing.

She'd always loved fishing.

Lara. Of all the unfortunate timing. To end up here when Mr. and Mrs. Ass-wipe were visiting for a fishing holiday. He should have just politely accepted the ride and chatted nonchalantly about how his life had changed so drastically, saying, "How wonderful you look!" and "How many kids do you have?" And "Why in the hell did you throw me over for that asshole?"

Puppy love. That's all it had been. But somehow, even though it was just puppy love, and even though they had parted as puppies, even though his current predicament should make an old relationship seem like a ridiculous waste of time and energy, he could still conjure up a damn good gut-wrenching ache when he let himself think about her and her betrayal. The years had dulled much of the pain, but sometimes, right in the early morning, just before the sun rose, Steve could still see her tranquil smile or the depth of her dark eyes and would reach out to touch the silky richness of her dark hair and feel that familiar tightness in his chest.

He had been extremely rude, so he could take solace in that. Or shame. But he'd owed her. Now maybe he could forget her completely. He had other things he needed to focus on.

The landscape lost its tranquil power as Steve continued to trudge toward…who knew where. Life was unbearable when you couldn't go home. At this moment he couldn't even risk calling his parents, whom he knew would be worried about him. He usually visited them on Sunday afternoons, and if he were out of town on business he would call. They hadn't heard from him in well over a month now, and he was nowhere near out of the woods. He couldn't risk sending them a message, or the next time they saw their son he could very easily be dead.

He was so damn tired—of sleeping on the ground, of eating out of a can, of looking over his shoulder. But thinking of how he had come to this point made him crazy, so he had to shift his thoughts to something else. Anything else.

The whine of rubber on pavement perked up his hopes. If he could just get a ride out of here…that would be something. Put some distance between him and Lara, if not between him and everything else.

He turned toward the oncoming truck and stuck his thumb in the air, and this time he got lucky. The blue Toyota stopped and a friendly, pretty, redheaded lady smiled out at him.

"I can't take you far," she said. "I'm just going to Ashton, but that'll at least save you thirty miles if you're staying on this road."

"That will be great. Thanks."

"You don't have to sit back there," the woman told Steve when he hoisted his guitar and pack into the backseat and then slid in next to them.

"Yes, I do, ma'am. I haven't had anything but a stream bath for days. I hope I don't offend you from here."

The lady's pleasant laughter filtered through him. It was so nice to hear the sound of another voice, especially a woman's. And he hadn't heard a laugh or laughed himself for a long, long time.

"My name's Jan Riley."

"Steve Mitchell," he replied.

"Where are you headed, Steve?"

He'd known this was coming. He'd prepared a lie, but Jan seemed so nice and sincere that he didn't feel like being dishonest. And he was so tired. "I'm…" He hesitated. "I'm not really sure."

"Are you looking for work?" the woman asked, gazing at him in her rearview mirror. Steve watched her reflection. Her eyes were the only part of her face that he could see, but they were definitely kind eyes, understanding and somewhat curious.

He took a moment to think. "I could use a job, Ms. Riley. Do you know of anyone needing help?"

"Have you ever done any carpentry work?"

"I can fix just about anything," he admitted.

"Good. Can you tend bar?"

"That's one thing I haven't done, but I'm sure I could learn."

"I need a handyman, but what I'm really looking for is a singer. Can you play that guitar you're carrying around?"

Steve felt his first twinge of uneasiness. Something in the recesses of his mind was throwing up a caution sign. But, singing in Ashton? Surely he could work a few weeks there without any consequences. That would give him some time to rest and decide what his next step would be. He had to go on the offensive eventually.

"I sing some," he admitted.

"Great. If you want a job, it's yours. I run Pond's Lodge. We rent cabins, have a little grocery store and a bar complete with a restaurant. You'll be expected to do just about anything we need during the day, and on Thursdays, Fridays, and Saturdays you'll do a three-set series of music. I've got a little cabin for you to stay in out back, and we serve some of the best food in the valley. I can only pay you a hundred and fifty dollars a week, but the deal includes room and board."

A wisp of suspicion wound through Steve's insides like a needle and thread darning a sock, but at this point he was so exhausted that he was willing to take the risk. A safe place to eat and sleep and even make some money? He didn't tell Jan, but he would have worked for room and board alone; that would give him a base of operations. He could already feel some of the tension easing from his shoulders. The arrangement would answer a forgotten prayer.

In Ashton, Jan turned into the parking lot of Dave's Market. She invited Steve to come in with her, but he shook his head.

"I'm going to be a while," she warned. "I've got to pick up some items that I don't sell in our little store. Are you sure you don't want to come in?"

"No, thank you," he said. "I'm too grubby. I think I'll just stay out here and sleep." And besides being dirty, Steve didn't want her to know he was so hungry he'd be tempted to steal something off the shelf.

"Fine," she said pleasantly. "I'll be about thirty minutes. Then we'll head back up to Island Park."

What? *What* had she just said? Steve felt the tension instantly return to every nerve in his body. Back to Island Park? Back toward Lara?

Oh, God. What had he got himself into?

Chapter Three

Lara leaned closer to the mirror and applied her mascara. Her hand was shaking so badly that she was afraid she might put her eye out.

It had been ten days since she called Jan on her cell phone and told her to pick up and hire "a hitchhiker she'd known from high school." She'd mentioned Steve was a wonderful singer, of course— Jan was looking for someone to sing in the bar and had been for over three weeks—but she hadn't said anything else. Her friend hadn't asked any questions or pushed for more information, either. When Lara told her the circumstances that day, Jan just hopped into action. That's why they were best friends. Well, that and because Jan had been seeing Lara's Uncle Lawrence since Lara's aunt's death five years earlier.

She was closer to Lawrence's age than Lara's own, but Jan was the complete opposite of uncle: boisterous, a blast to be around. Lara knew Lawrence was deeply in love with her, vibrant hair and personality and everything. He would sit in the back of a room and just watch her. She was so young at heart and full of energy that Lara felt as if there were no age difference between Jan and herself at all. Of course, nobody loved excitement and intrigue like Jan. She was a true romantic at heart, and she'd already told Lara she could "see the possibilities."

With Steve? Lara rolled her eyes. Romance wasn't even part of the picture. A romantic relationship wasn't in the cards for her again, not with anyone. Not after Phillip and that degradation. But she still wanted to apologize to Steve, to clear the air and move on with her life. That was all. And now, after ten days, she was going to make it happen.

She sighed and looked around her homey kitchen, dining, and living areas, and not without pride. She'd dreamed of owning a property along this stretch of river since childhood, and this enchanting cabin on the Buffalo was hers and hers alone. Several weeks after she'd returned to Island Park from California she heard that an older couple wanted to sell their home on the north bank, and she'd made a cash deal with them two days later, thankful for her divorce settlement: It bought her the home of her dreams far away from the chaos her former life had become, a place where she could rest and heal.

The lodge pole pine logs shone with a high gloss. She had kept the wood floors but added warm colors of Kelly green and mauve area rugs. Green plants filled every corner, and the unique leather furniture was accented with soft cushions in the same colors as the rugs. No curtains concealed her large windows. She had trees and wildflowers for a backyard, and a huge porch and the river for her front view.

Ninety percent of the time Lara's cabin reverberated with the strains of some haunting melody. Now the worn-out soundtrack from *The Man from Snowy River* echoed pure and clear from her CD player. Usually the piece soothed her. Tonight, as she thought of what lay ahead, the fluid movement of sound couldn't pacify the butterflies in her stomach.

Maybe the river could. The river was like a drug for her; it calmed her every time she gazed at it.

Stepping out onto the deck, Lara breathed in the heady fragrance of pines and flowers. Only a few feet below, the river gave her the tranquility she needed to gather her thoughts and prepare for her evening out.

The June night still held the hint of summer heat, and Lara soaked it in as she stared out over the water at Pond's Lodge. It was one of her favorite places to hang out when she just wanted to listen to music and have someone around who knew and cared about her.

Or it had been.

The lodge was built in 1923 and had changed owners over the years, but recently it had been purchased by Jan, who was a true visionary. Having lived in Island Park her entire life, Jan knew just how to turn Pond's into a very special destination. She'd poured her attention and money into the store and bar, knowing that the local crowd and visitors alike would spend most of their time there, just like at Lawrence's The TroutHunter down the river a bit.

Pond's was a family place. The bathrooms had been newly refurbished, as well the old ballroom, which held a bar at one end, an old stone fireplace on the back wall, high tables and chairs, and long low tables for larger groups. Jan had hired a chef from Utah. Andy was well known for his superb gourmet pizzas and melt-in-your-mouth French dip sandwiches. The long bar, so shiny you could see your face in it, was a great place to have a few beers and watch a football or baseball game on one of seven big-screen TVs. If you were one of the thousands of people who stopped in on their way to Yellowstone or Henry's Lake, you were welcomed as warmly as if you had been away from home for a very long time. Fishermen, utility workers, Fish and Game, people working with bear control or with wolves, store owners: everyone was treated like family. It was rare if the waitress didn't know your name and have your favorite drink poured before you sat down.

For the last ten days, Lara had found herself swallowing down a knot that rose like bile from her stomach whenever she thought of the place. Just knowing Steve was working there made her want to run away and hide. But she was a grown woman now, and she'd faced bigger demons since her time with Steve and would be damned if she wouldn't look this problem in the eye—or eyes; beautiful green eyes to be exact—tell him what she had to say and be done with this one unfinished thing in her life. Then she could heal.

Lara locked her doors and walked in the quickening darkness toward the lodge. As she neared, she could hear the soft strings of a guitar being smoothly strummed. The churning in her stomach returned, and she almost spun back toward her cabin, but the river played its own sweet song, promising that the time had come to take care of this situation.

The main entrance to the lodge opened into the lobby. The large glass windowpane had one simple word: SALOON. Lara quietly opened the door and slipped through to the interior unnoticed.

Instead of going to the bar like she usually did, she slid onto a tall wooden stool at the back. The bartender, Susan, was a friend of hers, and Susan nodded at her then looked over at Steve, then back again. Lara was suddenly sure Jan had filled the woman in on what she knew about their past.

Lara didn't dare turn her head in Steve's direction, although she faced the small stage where he played. And then she heard his natural and unique voice begin to sing.

"'Because I'm easy, yeah, because I'm easy.'"

Lara shut her eyes tight, hoping to drown out the sound, but his voice pulled at her, lured her toward him like one of the flies on the end of her lines would a fish. She opened her eyes and observed him fully for the first time in fifteen years, and…Steve Mitchell stared right through her.

Her breath caught in her throat. She wanted desperately to turn her head, but she knew if she did she would never dare attempt to defuse this explosive situation again. All she wanted was to tell him she was sorry for being such an ass and get on with her life. Was that so very horrible? Was it impossible for him to hear her say she was sorry?

Lara was suddenly conscious of the greenest of green eyes connected to her own. She had no idea what he was singing, and she guessed neither did he.

He looked toward another group of people. They were cheering loudly for him to sing another song, so Lara took the moment to really look him over. She was startled to find that he had transformed into a magnificent man. Gone was the road dust and grease. His long dark hair was pulled back in a silky ponytail, and a soft-looking beard and mustache shadowed his face, giving him a lean and angular look. In the last fifteen years his body had filled out considerably, with thick shoulders and thighs, muscles toned to perfection under a western shirt that matched the green of his eyes. Lara found herself wanting very much for him to stand up and turn around so that she could see the rest.

Her eyes traveled up and down those six feet of masculinity. God, he looked good. Better than she remembered. Better than she'd imagined. Much better than she wanted him to look. She would have thought someone down on his luck would look withered and skinny, but here in Pond's Lodge he looked like he'd walked straight out of a gym.

And his *voice.* It cut through her like a hot knife. For a brief moment she was sixteen years old once more, sitting close to an outdoor fire and even closer to Steve, her head resting on his shoulder as he strummed a soft love song. Oh, how she'd shared his love for the music, and her rich alto harmony had made the two a perfect match.

His song ended and he started another. These lyrics spoke of love, but as Lara looked into his eyes she read the bitterness she'd noticed when she tried to give him a ride. No, Steve Mitchell wasn't singing his love song to her, and she knew it.

The longer he continued, the worse Lara's nerves got. Susan had long since set a glass of Chardonnay in front of her, which she hadn't touched. Any time now, Steve would have a break and the moment of reckoning would be upon her.

Why. She wanted to tell him why she had dumped him without a backwards glance, but now, as she looked at him with a woman's eyes, she couldn't for the life of her remember. How could she have been so stupid? The thought of trading Steve for Philip seemed ludicrous. At this very moment Lara didn't know what had happened to Steve after they broke, but seeing him reminded her of all that she'd loved about him in the first place. She knew what kind of a person he'd been, and she didn't believe anyone could change that much, not even in fifteen years.

Or could he? She sure as hell had.

* * *

Steve had no idea what he was singing. His fingers kept picking over the strings, his voice sang the lyrics, but he had no clue as to what was coming out. Why in the hell didn't she get out of here? And where was Mr. Ass-wipe? He had hoped and prayed that her vacation was over by now and she'd returned to wherever she lived. He'd been focusing on what he was in the area to do. Not that he'd had much luck.

She looked so damn beautiful and out of place in the noisy barroom, he had feared he wouldn't be able to sing around the knot in his throat when she sat down. Lara's surroundings should be open air and sunshine. Her shiny dark hair was still long after all these years, but she wore it wilder and freer. Sexier. Her skin still seemed to glow, especially against the purple of her blouse. He had always loved that perfect complexion. There had never been a time when he was close enough to touch her that he hadn't raised a finger to that cheek.

She'd been prone to soft smiles in the past, but he hadn't seen one tonight. She looked similar to the girl he had loved, but those hazel eyes held a seriousness that he didn't remember; a grown-up concern clouded her features, and there was a determination in the tilt of her chin that threw him for a loop. What in the hell was she doing here? He'd thought he made it perfectly clear when he met her on the road that he wanted absolutely nothing to do with her. And not just because of what she'd done to him. Shit, even speaking to her could put her at risk. He was a walking time bomb.

There was an easy enough way to fix this.

"Ladies and gentlemen," he said into the mic, shaking off thoughts of his current predicament. "I'm going to take a quick break and wet my whistle. I'll be back in five."

He hurried from the low stage and went behind the bar. "Susan," he whispered to the bartender. "See that lady in the back with the purple top?"

Susan didn't even turn. "You mean Lara?"

"Do you know her?" Steve was surprised.

"Sure, everybody does. What about her?"

"Will you please go tell her to find another bar to drink in? I don't want her around me."

Susan glanced over. "I can't do that, Steve. She's a local here, and we all love her to death."

"A local? You mean she lives here year-round?"

"Yep."

"Oh, God." He shook his head. "Pour me a beer, please."

She did, and when he went back to the stage he steered away from songs of the past or anything that might remind him of their days together.

Lara Douglas. Mrs. Ass-wipe. The woman was extremely bad news as far as he was concerned. God, how he wanted her to leave the lodge. He needed another drink, and his fingers felt like they were picking at razor blades, but if he took another break he would *have* to walk over there and be polite, and he'd be damned if he was going to set himself up for a fall that like that again. He wasn't stupid enough to lay his hand on the same burner twice.

Besides, he shouldn't be seen talking to her, he reminded himself again. She didn't know it, but there were people out there that might do more than *love* her to death if she had anything to do with him.

He couldn't afford to have any friends right now. Not if he valued their safety or his own. Not if he wanted to succeed in his task, finish this whole debacle and return to his life.

Unfortunately, right after he finished his next song, Jan stepped in front of the microphone. "Steve will be taking a short break," she said, "so get your drinks freshened and he'll be back in fifteen minutes."

The owner of Pond's Lodge turned to face him then, a knowing look in her eye. "She's a stubborn one, Steve. You might as well get it over with."

Steve was stunned. How did Jan know anything about his former relationship with Lara? And if Jan knew, who else did? That was all he needed right now, everybody in town bringing up his name. This woman caused as much distress as a person could in his life, and she would create some truly serious problems for him if she didn't keep her mouth shut. So he intended to tell her just that.

Resting his guitar on his stool, Steve took the Corona Jan had brought him. After a long gulp, he walked briskly over to where Lara sat at a small table by herself, pulled a high-back chair out and turned it around, straddling it backwards. Maybe the slats would give him the protection he needed to stay clear of this gorgeous piece of trouble. After all these years he still felt an inescapable draw.

Actually, now that he sat inches from her face, he could tell that she was scared to death. There was none of the high and mighty sophistication he'd expected after her marriage to that rich bastard Philip.

He made sure his voice showed his irritation. He did not want this to get even remotely friendly. "What do you want, Lara?"

She visibly flinched, but he held himself steady.

"I…" She faltered. "How have you been, Steve?"

He didn't answer her. *Don't let the sincerity act fool you, ol' man. You've dealt with better liars than this.*

"We've got to get out of here," he said with a harshness he didn't quite feel. "Meet me in three minutes in Jan's office. Do you know where that is?"

Lara nodded without speaking, so Steve rose abruptly and exited the bar through a side door. Going into Jan's office, he stood behind the desk and waited. He tried to slow his breathing and get a grip on his emotions. To be honest, no matter what he told himself, he'd thought of little else besides her for the past ten days. Still, whatever her story, he knew that for his own good as well as hers he had to make her never want to see him again.

The office door opened and she peeked her head around it. Jan's desk lamp was the only light, as Steve had turned it on.

"Did anyone follow you?" he blurted.

"No, why would someone be following me?" Lara asked.

"That just goes to show that what you don't know can hurt you."

She looked mystified. "Okay, Steve, I give. What do I need to know that can hurt me?"

Steve was a little taken aback at her suddenly steady gaze and the stubborn sarcasm in her voice. This was new from Lara. She had more edge than he remembered, and in some crazy way he liked it. Still, he had to make his next statements precise, leaving her no room to question.

"I don't have the time or the patience for your bullshit. You made yourself perfectly clear fifteen years ago that you were choosing another path, and now I've moved on. You're not wanted or needed in my world, Lara. I don't require your help or sympathy or any of your shit. I don't know any details of your life since we parted, and I don't want to know them. Not now, not ever. Any questions?"

His gut twisted as he spoke, but he held his body erect and stern. He knew Lara and saw how his words were cutting into her. Still, this was best for them both, regardless of his insane desire to rush forward and hold her and tell her how much he'd missed her. But he couldn't. He wouldn't. And with a slight nod, Lara was gone.

She moved silently from the room. Steve immediately shut off the lamp and followed, hurrying from the darkness, afraid that if he stayed a second longer he would succumb to the grief that gripped his heart like nothing else in the past fifteen years.

Once again, they were over.

Chapter Four

Lara wandered back to her cabin, stumbling randomly as if drunk. Steve's words had been worse than stabs to her heart. Each seemed to grow like ripples in a pond, larger and larger, more and more awful. *Patience...bullshit...chose another path...moved on...* Each word was a wound. *Don't want or need you... Don't want to know....*

With shaky hands she took her house key from her pocket and opened her door. For the first time since she'd moved here, she was frightened by the shadows in the corners. She rushed through the house turning on every light, and only after she checked everywhere thoroughly did she pour herself a glass of wine. Pulling a fleece blanket around herself, she stared at nothing.

After three sips of wine, she felt her tension ease and her brain began to clear. What was she frightened of? Did she think Steve would hurt her? No, of course not. That wasn't it. So what had her on such edge that she was searching the shadows? Had it simply been the fury in his face when he said that what she didn't know could hurt her? Or was it simply that she'd hoped for something more from him?

After the full glass of wine she felt a little like her old self. She walked to the bathroom, used the toilet and then stood to wash her hands. Her beautifully hand-carved mirror stood over the sink in front of her. Usually, as she did her makeup, she would admire the craftsmanship of a solitary lodge pole pine tree carved along the side and the bear across the top, but tonight she only stared at her face, shock still covering her skin like the grey dust from a dirt road.

Seriously, though, what had she expected? Casual conversation? *"Hi, Steve, how's life been treating you?"* Or maybe, *"You look great, Lara. Better than ever. How have you been all these years?"*

Really, when she stopped to think about it, Steve had let her know his position the first time he saw her again. How stupid could she be? Had she thought he would change his mind about her in the last ten days? What possible reason would there be for that? Once again she wished she knew about his life since college. He'd been there one day and gone the next, and then she'd had her own crises to deal with.

She slept terribly, and just before light, after a night of tossing and turning, she finally got dressed, made coffee, put on a warm jacket and slipped out into the dawn to get ready for her fly-fishing lesson with Dr. Carson. As she walked to the jeep, however, she couldn't get Steve's green eyes out of her mind. Intense, brooding, angry... Yes. But there had been something more.

Fear. That was it. She still had no idea what was going on with Steve, but instinctively she knew there'd been more to his speech than just the fact that he didn't want her in his life. So, there was something else going on. She was positive. Seriously, Steve's reaction to her had been overly dramatic. He'd left her no room to speak; she didn't even remember him taking a breath. So, what in the hell was going on? Steve might hate her—and she couldn't blame him; she'd let him down, very harshly down—but he'd had a desperate look about him at the lodge. She couldn't be the cause of that, not fifteen years later. Not even if he'd kept her in his thoughts as a *what-if* like she had him.

So, what exactly was Steve Mitchell afraid of?

They had known each other's every thought, every action in high school. They'd first met when her teacher Mr. Mathews suggested Lara find someone in class who better understood algebra to help her with assignments. She could still remember the leather jacket Steve wore when he shyly came up to her locker after class and offered to help. Her first reaction had been to say no thanks, he wasn't one of her crowd and didn't fit with the clean-cut church-going boys that she was used to dating, but then she'd looked up into those deep green eyes and was stunned to silence. They'd held an intensity she'd never seen before, and as he stood shifting his books from one hand to the other she'd suddenly realized what it took for Steve to step out of his comfort zone and offer his help.

She'd graciously accepted. After that, an innocent and wholesome love developed. At first they'd met only in the library after school, but then she traded seats with another girl so she could sit next to him in class. It wasn't long before he was invited to her home for dinner, and her father had been impressed with Steve's quiet and respectful presence.

They'd found they shared a love for music, especially '60s and '70s rock-and-roll. Steve started bringing over his guitar, and late that summer they started a small band with another guitarist and a drummer. They'd set up a practice space in Steve's parents' garage, where Steve's mom would always show up with a snack and sodas. On long Saturday rehearsals she'd bring them sandwiches, and after they took a break for lunch Mrs. Mitchell would stay and listen, praise and gently direct them with sound advice, since she too had a passion for music, which she'd abandoned to raise a family.

As Lara's mother was killed in a car accident when she was six, Steve's mother became like a mom to Lara. She helped Lara design some outfits for the band, and in their junior year she took Lara shopping for a dress for the prom. Steve was Lara's date, of course, and the night of the prom they performed the theme song for their classmates. That night Lara talked Steve into joining her in a Spanish class the next year, and they'd learned the language together. Near the end of senior year they took a trip to Mexico with the Spanish Club…and that's where she'd bought Steve the Cozumel sticker for his guitar case.

Lara shivered. They'd had so many wonderful times together, through those years in high school and then their first year in college. It was crazy to think how they were different people now, had lived separate lives. But if he thought he could just dismiss her like that, dismiss all that they'd shared, he was wrong. He might have known her then, but he didn't know her now. Her life with Philip had forced her to grow up, to work out her problems and hit them head-on.

No, Steve didn't know the new Lara Douglas. She'd trained herself to wear a thick skin when it came to matters of the heart. She would don her coat of armor once more and walk into battle, head held high. She would find out more about Steve's life and then tell him exactly how she felt about him, all before he left Island Park. Yes, she would tell him how she felt…just as soon as she figured it out for herself.

But Steve was in some kind of trouble and didn't want her near him. Did she really have the right to ignore that?

* * *

By six-thirty a.m. Dr. Carson had eaten his usual hearty breakfast of pancakes, eggs, sausage, and hash browns, and he was already in his neoprene waders and fly-fishing vest. As he arrived Lara noticed a flush to his blotchy cheeks, and she realized that in the last ten days he had let himself get sunburned.

"Dr. Carson, you really should keep your hat on. You, better than many, should know the hazards of skin cancer."

He chuckled. "I know you're right, Lara, but I'm usually either in my office or an operating room, and the sun feels so good and the air so clean here, I hate to miss a minute of it."

"I hear you, Doc, but your bald spot is as bright as an apple. Put your hat on and keep it there all day or I'm not taking you downriver."

Lara grinned as she scolded him. He knew she was kidding. They had connected right away and become fast friends, despite the fact that she'd briefly abandoned him in her failed attempt to talk to Steve. Doc was a quick learner, and he'd had so much fun learning the basics of fly-fishing in the slower water that Lara now felt he was ready for a faster part of the river. When she'd surprised him yesterday with the news, she'd felt like Santa. Doc had seemed like a kid on Christmas morning, and although nearing seventy, he still looked that way.

"I'm going to take you to a favorite place of mine, but if you ever tell anyone where it is I'll have to shoot you. Got it?" she said.

Doc nodded, but in her mind Lara heard Steve's final words to her last night. *"Any questions?"* She had to take a moment to shake off her upset.

To hell with Steve Mitchell, she told herself, especially now. She had a gorgeous, cloudless day of fishing ahead with a very attentive student, and she'd be damned if that jerk would ruin a perfect time on the river for her. She'd erase him from her mind until tonight, when she would shock the shit out of him by showing up again at Pond's. No matter what he'd said, she wasn't giving up. But that was tonight. For now she was Doc's and only Doc's.

In less than twenty minutes they were both standing on a different bank of Henry's Fork. Here the current moved at a pace much faster than Doc had fished up until today, and Lara could sense his uncertainty as soon as she turned to look at him. The danger of this part of the river was heightened. She knew instinctively that she must change tactics, adopt a more philosophical way of approaching his apprehension.

"Doc, today we are going to learn the *art* of fly-fishing. No more technique. What you learn today will make a world of difference."

He nodded but didn't say anything, so she untied the red bandana she usually wore around her neck and stepped behind him.

"I'm going to cover your eyes," she said. Then she assured him, "Don't worry, I'm not going to have you get in the water blindfolded." She tied the hanky so it was lightly covering his eyes. "Okay?"

He nodded.

"Now, I want you to see in your mind's eye what you imagine to be the very best outcome you can possibly imagine while fishing today. Feel the rod in your right hand, the texture of the handle, and your left hand holding the line. All without picking anything up. Can you feel it? Can you see it?"

"Yes."

"Good. Now, in perfect timing look at the river and watch for all the small things you've learned this past week. Do you know what you're looking for?"

"Yes," said Dr. Carter. "I can see the movement, bigger rocks, flies floating on the surface, and a rainbow trout lifting its mouth to take one in."

"Perfect. Now, I want you to see yourself stepping into this swifter current. Feel the water tug at your waders, the slippery rocks beneath your boots. Do you know what you must do now that you're in the water before anything else?"

The doctor changed the position of his feet, firmly planting them.

"You remembered," Lara stated, quietly pleased. "Good. What is the first word in fly-fishing?"

"Balance."

"Balance is the number one rule—in any sport, really. You can't swing a bat or serve a tennis ball without balance, right?" She took a moment for the doctor to process then said, "Next I want you to see exactly where you want your fly to settle. Have you placed it floating downstream, just as a real fly would float? Have you got your rhythm down just the way you want it?"

"Rhythm," the doctor repeated, almost as if hypnotized.

"You must keep your rhythm or you'll lose the confidence you must bring to the water. Always remember, your timing is unlike anyone else's in the world. Your rhythm is as unique to you as what you do in the operating room. Now, throw out a few more times and tell me when something interesting happens."

Lara paused, letting him cast in his mind for a time. In the silence, though, she suddenly heard her very own words, really heard them for the first time, the same words she'd been using to teach hundreds of students over the years, about seeing the perfect outcome. About finding balance. About personal timing. And the last two lessons she hadn't yet mentioned to the doctor were important too.

"I've got him!" the doctor yelled, pulling her out of her thoughts.

"What?" she said dumbly.

"I've got a four-pounder on the line!"

The doctor was still standing on the bank, the bandana wrapped across his eyes, acting like he was holding on to his pole for dear life as if he truly did have a trout on the hook.

Lara giggled as she removed his mask. "You, Doc, have got to be the best student I've ever had. So, what are the last two lessons after balance and rhythm? Remind me."

The doctor lifted his chin toward the early morning sunshine and whispered, "'Keep your tip up,' and last but never least, 'Have patience.'"

That's right, Lara thought. *You let the fish come to you.*

"You know, Lara," Dr. Carter continued, "it's all about timing. For over thirty years I've been tying flies to keep my fingers nimble for surgery, but it was only this year I finally forced myself to leave my practice for a month to fulfill this lifelong dream. And you are the best instructor I could have possibly asked for. Thank you."

"Oh, believe me, Doc," she said, "it's been my pleasure."

Dr. Carter looked down at his hands, which he still clenched like he held a pole and a fishing line. "Visualizing like this. It's similar to what I do in the operating room. Our professions are really sort of similar."

Lara laughed. "I would never want to venture into your realm and try to do what you do on a daily basis. My life isn't near as important as yours."

"Oh, but it is, my dear," said the doctor. "And don't let anyone ever tell you otherwise. Don't take anything away from this. A person can find his soul here, in your valley. Never forget the importance of such a wonderful gift. I may be able to give a patient a new lease on life, but I have never been able to heal a broken soul. You can, Lara, you have that capacity. And it's not just this spiritual place but your spirit as well."

Lara glanced at him, and he smiled. She wasn't sure how to respond.

"You're a naturally nurturing human being, Lara Douglas. If I might ask a personal question, why have you never married?"

The question threw her completely off her guard, and she blurted the truth before she could think. "I was once, but he turned out to be nothing like I thought. And there was another man, but... Never mind."

"Aw," said the doctor, clearly sympathizing. Then: "You've given me so much good advice, would you mind if I share a little piece of my own?"

Lara shrugged. "Of course not."

"I'm no psychic, but I've noticed a sad longing in your eyes since the first day we met. Don't get me wrong, you've been most gracious and fun to be with, and I've enjoyed your company immensely, but the sadness lingers. This morning, I thought you might be ill. You looked so downhearted. So, Lara Douglas, whatever is bothering you, take care of it one way or another. Put it to rest. Take it from an old bachelor who always put work above everything. Nothing, not even the beauty of Island Park, can fix words left unspoken and actions not taken."

Chapter Five

Lara sat on her deck that evening, loving the way the waning sun perfectly lit the trees and river, her river, her home, this small but impossibly beautiful place in the world.

On the rail of her porch, a vivid Steller's jay nibbled at the wild birdseed she sprinkled every morning and again each night after work. She watched the jay in all his majestic blue brilliance, with his black head and tiny Mohawk. He was king here—right now anyway, until an osprey or eagle decided to give him a little competition. The eagle, whose nest sat on the rugged edge of the falls further down, only came once in a while to irritate him, preferring to eat squirrel or rabbit or fish. The osprey too, preferred meat, but if it came down to a fight the jay might just give him a good one. In the right mood he could rattle pinecones from the trees with his chattering.

Lara fed sparrows as well, and chipmunks and squirrels, but other than her Steller's jay, her very favorite animals were the fat little black and grey chickadees with their white bellies. She never tired of watching nature, and always after seeing something rare or new she would return to her computer and learn everything she could about it. Dr. Carson had been right. This was a place of both learning and rebirth.

Glancing at her phone, she noticed it was only six-thirty. She still had well over two hours before she would crank up her courage and go to the bar to hear Steve sing. She'd called Jan first thing after Doc left—he planned to rest in his room before dinner—who confirmed that Steve hadn't quit his job last night. But he apparently hadn't said two words to anyone all day, either. Frankly, Jan added, no one wanted to talk to him, since his stormy demeanor kept everyone at bay.

Lara leaned her head back against her Adirondack cushioned chair and took a deep long breath. *Breathe in, breathe out.* She thought back to late that afternoon, and to how Doc had conquered his fear of the faster current and ended the day with the biggest catch of the week for The TroutHunter. Lara had snapped a picture of him proudly holding a five-and-a-half pound German brown trout before he proudly released it back into the water for some other fisherman to enjoy catching.

Fly-fishing. It was known as the gentleman's sport—or, as in her case, as well as in the cases of many females all over the world, the gentle*woman's* sport. The object was to tempt the fish, lure him to the bait, tease him with what he couldn't have until he was pissed off enough to grab at it. It wasn't about keeping the fish and frying it up for dinner, although they were delicious, but this stretch of the Snake was catch-and-release.

Hmmm, that gave Lara a plan for tonight.

* * *

In his room behind the lodge, Steve breathed a sigh of relief. He hadn't seen Lara all day. He'd been afraid that she would come back demanding an explanation, especially since his delivery had been a bit incoherent last night. After going to his room he'd thought of a lot of other things he should have said, awful things that she still deserved to hear. He hoped she'd heard the distaste in his voice so that she wouldn't come back for more, or he would give it to her with both barrels and then some.

It seemed his ploy had worked, though. He hadn't seen her since. Unfortunately, for the sake of everyone involved, for Jan and for the other workers at the lodge, for Lara and himself, it was probably time to be moving on.

It would be sad. Despite the fact that he hadn't gotten much of his original goal accomplished, Steve had been pleased with his brief stint here. Jan had told him he was good enough to have a singing career and that she hoped she could help him toward that goal with the exposure; she didn't know he had a career of his own that was…successful in its way if not as enjoyable.

She'd had new posters made of his singing engagements through the 4th of July, so that weekend would be his last—if something didn't happen beforehand. Jan had been so proud of that poster, and of him, her first official guest singer, but she had no idea that putting his name up there might alert his would-be killers. And they *were* that. Steve had no illusion that they would stop at anything to see him gone forever, along with anyone else who got in the way. He just had to be sure he saw them coming.

He lifted his backpack and set it on the bed. This tiny log room was big enough only for a single, and for one hardwood chair and a small table with a lamp. A rustic stone fireplace was a smaller replica of the one in the main lodge. An updated bathroom had been a pleasant surprise. When Steve first walked in after a month of hiding out in the mountains, it had seemed like a palace. Now the tight space was a little too confining. And he had an anticipation of doom, especially after work every day when he had no other place to go and nothing to do.

He'd already read every book in Jan's little collection. She'd started bringing him volumes she'd checked out from the town library, and he practiced his guitar until the tips of his fingers bled. Nevertheless he was itchy, ready to be back in a familiar territory where he had more of a chance of survival than he had here.

He rummaged through the few supplies he would take if he had to leave on foot again, checked to see if his 9mm was fully loaded and if he still had the two extra clips hidden in an old boot. He pulled a board from the ceiling that he'd pried off his first night and shoved the pack into the hole and reattached the board. Then he showered and trimmed his beard and mustache.

He was finally getting used to this gruff new look. The beard had finally quit itching; besides, it gave him some small sense of security, of disguise from the former person he'd been. It also gave him a bit of strength to keep up his crusty persona.

After pulling on a clean pair of jeans and—ironed, thanks to Jan—navy plaid western shirt, he picked up his guitar and left, locked his door and walked the few steps to the side door of Pond's. The place was already half full, many guests eating a late dinner after fishing or floating along one of the many rivers and streams that were popular attractions in the area. Some people were still in their fishing attire, others in cutoffs and t-shirts. Others still were dressed up to spend a night drinking and dancing to some good old-time music. Jan had told Steve business picked up after he started singing, but tonight was the first time he truly believed her.

Hurriedly he set up his mic, deciding that he would give this crowd an early set and maybe some of them would bring their friends back later in the evening when the joint was really rocking. If he could help Jan earn some extra money while he was here, that was the least he could do. The woman had given him a place to rest and recuperate.

He started with an old Beach Boys tune that always got the crowd's motor running, even if some were too young to have ever heard it before. Using the back of his guitar to start a drum beat, he zoomed into, "'She's so fine, my 409.'"

Even an octave lower than Brian Wilson would have sung it, the melody carried him and a crowd was dancing before Steve was done, from young to old, leaving their food forgotten on their plates. He whizzed through another half dozen songs before he stopped for a break, and by the time he finished his second set there wasn't room to stand. Jan handed him a Corona as he stepped behind the bar. She was grinning from ear to ear, pouring drink after drink for her happy customers.

"Do you know what I love most about tonight, Steve?" she questioned.

"That you've got a great crowd and they are buying lots of booze?"

"No, that's not it at all. Look around you. Everyone is happy and having such a great time, and it's not just because of the liquor. It's so much more than that. This minute—this *hour*—is a dream I've had since I was a teenager, and at sixty I'm finally seeing it come true." She paused and stared at him. "You should never give up on your dreams, Steve, no matter how far away they seem."

There had been a time in Steve's life when his biggest dream was to create music and make it his career. He'd always felt better playing and writing. He and Lara had spent hours sharing dreams of a life on the road, touring and singing, writing music together, having a quirky little family. But all dreams didn't come true, and theirs was one of those to fail.

He didn't say anything, so Jan continued, "The winters are long and cold up here, and many times we are snowbound, but now we will have this night and many like it to carry us through. Thanks for sharing your talents with us, Steve. I'll always remember this as one of the highlights of my life. Now, get back out there. You have two more sets, and this crowd is hungry for more."

He began the next set with a slow dance, and thinking of Lara he sang an Alabama song, "The Closer You Get," watching couples step into small places and back corners of the dancehall. "'The further I fall,'" he sang with his eyes shut, remembering against his better judgment the way her low and silky voice gave a perfect harmony behind him when they were teens, and when he opened his eyes she was there.

At first he thought he was imagining her, because she had the same color sundress that he'd loved the very most when they were together. It was sage green, and it had spaghetti straps, a term she'd taught him when they were juniors in high school. He remembered her walking down the stairs of her parents' house as he stood waiting in the entryway, an orchid corsage in his left hand shaking like a leaf in the wind as he watched her descend like an angel dressed in lavender.

She looked straight at him now, with absolutely none of the timidity she'd shown in high school or the quiet defeat he'd seen last night as she walked out of Jan's office. *Dear God,* he prayed, while never missing a lick or a lyric of the song he'd been singing about her and only her for the past fifteen years. *Please make her go away. Please.*

But Lara didn't leave, and the couples, all dreamy-eyed for their significant others, were soon waiting for another slow song.

It was funny, he told himself. He'd been one of these couples back in high school and college. He'd loved dancing, had praised the person who first invented it, for what other way could you hold someone so close that you could smell the fresh scent of her hair, touch her cheek, and press her breasts into your chest, without seeming vulgar? What other way could—?

Snap the fuck out of this, Steve, he told himself. What kind of witch's spell had she cast over him that she still affected his thoughts and body so many years later? But there was a counter-spell. He had only to stop and think of that rainy Saturday in college to force his heart back to reality.

Looking at the crowd, he racked his brain to find a slow song that would not have lyrics too intimate, too telling about what was really going through his mind. After several seconds he settled on Willie Nelson's, "To All the Girls." Hopefully she would believe that she was only one of many he'd loved, regardless of how far that was from the truth.

He saw an older couple at the far end of the bar wave goodbye to Jan, and as they left they motioned to Lara that a seat was available. She took it, and though it was the farthest space from where he was performing, it confirmed that she wasn't leaving. Damn it!

He revved things back up with four lively songs, ending with the old but ever-popular "Boot-Scootin' Boogie." Most of the men took this time to order another beer, but almost every lady in the place hit the floor. Jan threw her bar towel down, went around the bar, and dragged Lara into a line dance, and it was then that Steve first noticed Lara's footwear. He'd never known her to wear cowboy boots, and with that little sundress those brown and turquoise boots looked sexy as hell.

He was able to watch her this time, as her back was to him. God, but she had grown up in all the right places. The line dance required a turn in all four directions, so he got a great look at her ass and then a side view of her curvaceous bus-line, but the next turn had her facing him. He tried to keep his eyes on her boots, but for the life of him he couldn't.

His gaze slid up to her slim waist, and he wondered if she'd had children. The thought made his jaw clench, so he looked further up, at her full breasts, then past the shadow of cleavage to that creamy complexion... He should have kept looking at her boobs, because soon he saw that gorgeous mouth that he remembered so well and then her whole face. Still so very beautiful.

She never lifted her eyes to look at him, and although the dance was fast and fun she didn't smile or look like she was enjoying herself. Steve wasn't enjoying himself, either, but he was professional enough to fake it for the audience.

Just as the song was about to end, Lara rushed back to her seat. Steve played one more. He usually never did seven songs in a row, but this time he needed the extra three or four minutes to compose himself and decide what to do about this new twist of fate.

Fate? Shit, this had nothing to do with fate. Lara had simply come back after all the things he'd said to her. What was she doing?

"Time for me to take a break, I'll be back in fifteen minutes," he told the crowd.

He left the hall for the bathroom, and after he got rid of the beer he'd drunk earlier he washed his hands and face in the sink and smoothed back his long hair with a wet hand. "Pull it together, buddy," he told himself out loud. "Get out there and finish this once and for all."

Steve hoped his determined stride showed more confidence than he felt. He walked directly to Lara, who was sitting once again at the end of the bar. He took the chair next to her, and the bartender quickly brought him a Corona. She looked nervous.

"Thanks, Susan," he said. "Could you get me a shot of whisky, too?"

"Sure," the bartender said. "Lara, can I get you anything?"

Steve looked over at her, and Lara asked boldly, "Are you buying?"

"Sure," he said. "Whatever."

Neither spoke while Susan poured. She set the two double whiskies down and quickly moved to the other end of the bar.

Steve took half of his in one gulp and then turned to Lara. She downed half of hers as well, and with watering eyes she confronted him square-on. Steve wanted to grin because it was obvious she wasn't used to drinking whisky, but he didn't. Still, now that he'd had some liquid courage, he was ready to give it to her.

"What do you want from me, Lara? You look great. Better than ever. Is that what you wanted to hear? You do." He hesitated briefly then started again. "Lara, we knew each other a lifetime ago. I'm sure you haven't thought of me for more than ten seconds since the day I walked out of your room, and Lord knows I haven't been pining over you. So let's cut the crap. Why do you keep bothering me here? What do you want?"

The warmth in her eyes, deep green with brown flecks, grew dimmer with each word he uttered. He watched that fire die, knew what he was doing to her but couldn't stop himself. He wanted to hurt her back, wanted her to feel a tenth of what his gut suffered every time he thought about her. There were all the other reasons he couldn't get close to anyone right now, too. It just wasn't safe.

Tears welled in her eyes, and this time he knew it wasn't the burn of whisky down her throat. "Maybe I should ask you the same thing, Steve. What do you want from me? Why are you hanging around here when you know this is my home and has been for years? I know damn well it isn't for the job. You could work anywhere, so what's keeping you here?"

"Well, I didn't know you lived in Island Park until Susan told me last night," Steve admitted, and he saw her surprise. "I thought you must be vacationing here."

She hesitated for a split second and then stood, took her glass of whisky and swigged the last of it in one gulp. When she moved within inches of his face, he could smell sunshine mixed with liquor. This time there were no watery eyes; that water had turned to pure fire. "If you don't want me in your life, fine, no problem. *You* leave!"

She slammed her glass down so hard that everyone along the bar turned to look. She raised her chin then, and with purposeful steps and a straight back opened the door and walked into the darkness.

Steve stared after her until Jan announced him again. Then he picked up his guitar and sang the songs of the past. Each was more emotional than the last, and every one was dedicated silently to the one and only woman he had ever loved.

Lara.

Chapter Six

Sunday was like any business day at The TroutHunter. Some of the guests had checked out of their rooms and were packing their belongings; others were mingling in the lobby buying souvenirs. Lara's Uncle Lawrence had already left to work a day-long float trip.

Lara noticed that the resort's supply of elk-hair caddis flies was getting low. Not surprising, as the trout had been taking them extremely well the past week. She had just sat down at a log table to begin tying when Jan walked in.

Her friend didn't waste any time with preliminaries. "What happened last night?"

"Nothing," Lara said.

"He came over to talk to you. I saw that much. I was working the other end of the bar, so I couldn't hear the conversation."

"There was very little, Jan. He simply told me that he didn't want anything to do with me." Lara put down her dry fly and stared at the table. "I only want to apologize for the past, but he won't let me."

"He's feeling more than he's letting on, Lara. Believe me. After you left, he sang a string of love songs from the late eighties and early nineties that would have ripped your heart out. He was remembering, there's no doubt in my mind. How close were you two? And what the hell happened?" She eyed Lara. "I can't imagine any woman in her right mind letting that gorgeous man go."

Lara shook her head and then saw a customer waiting patiently at the counter to pay for a sweatshirt with the TroutHunter logo, and a few others were waiting to check out. "I'll be right back."

As she rang the first woman up, Lara wondered if she could tell Jan the whole story. She'd never given anyone all the details. Maybe it would help to talk it out. Maybe it wouldn't seem quite so terrible after all these years.

Maybe.

She made a decision. Smiling weakly at her last customer, Lara thanked her then said goodbye before calling a teenage boy who lived nearby and worked for her and her uncle during summers.

"Ryan," she asked when he picked up the phone, "can you come hold down the fort for a little while? I think everyone has checked out for today, so it should be pretty quiet for an hour or so before any new customers start arriving."

"Sure, Lara. No problem," Ryan said.

When he arrived, Lara walked to the bar, grabbed two beers and walked slowly back to Jan. "Let's go out to the deck," she told her friend. "We'll have privacy out there."

There were tables and chairs along the width of the lodge overlooking the Snake. The river stretched long and languid, and swans lingered below in the shallow water. Both women sipped their Coronas for a few minutes before Lara began to tell her story.

"Steve and I met my sophomore year at high school, in algebra. I lived in Gilbert, Arizona. He had just transferred from California. He was the smartest kid in the class, and I was failing. He offered to help me, and he did. For the next three years we were inseparable.

"I should explain my upbringing before I tell you the rest," she decided, not looking at Jan as she continued. "I was born into a religious family. We went to church every Sunday, and I was always taught that sex was out of the question until I married. I believed in my dad's counsel, and in my church leaders.

"Steve came from a more laidback lifestyle. He had a couple of older brothers, and his parents taught him about safe-sex, but that's as far as they interfered. So, the first time we went a little beyond kissing and I stopped him and explained what I truly believed, you could tell by his expression that he thought it was a bunch of bullshit. But he loved me. We made a pact that night that we would wait until our wedding night. He promised to go along with my wishes because that's what I felt was right for me."

Lara looked up at Jan and took a long swig of her beer. "I know," she said before her friend could speak. "It sounds pretty damn old-fashioned to me now, but I thought every 'good' girl was doing the same thing."

Jan said nothing, just wore an expression of sympathy. Lara loved her all the more for it.

"Anyway, by the end of our senior year everyone expected us to get married, including us. Then we went to Mexico on vacation with the Spanish Club, and after a long talk we decided to get some more education before we got tied down. However, I couldn't stand the thought of us being apart, so we both went to San Diego State.

"Our first year in college, many times, we both almost gave in to desire, but somehow we managed to keep our commitment. More times than not it was Steve who was strong. He used to tell me that if he surrendered we would always regret it, and that he respected my decision above all." Lara could feel a tight knot blocking off her air, but she fought her way through it and added, "He used to tell me often that I was worth waiting for."

Jan nodded but still said nothing. Lara shifted uncomfortably in her chair, twisted to stare at a red-tail hawk floating above the lodge, and continued. It was getting harder.

"My roommate introduced me to a guy named Philip Barnhart. He was a senior, the student-body president and very good-looking. He was blond and blue-eyed. He had a lean, powerful body, and he liked me. All of my new friends told me I was crazy if I didn't go out with him. Every girl at school wanted that chance, and there I was turning it down. So, it wasn't very long before I started rationalizing: Shouldn't I know for sure if Steve was the man I wanted to spend the rest of my life with? Wasn't that one reason we'd come to school?" Lara hesitated in her story. "I need another beer. Would you like one?"

"Sure," Jan said. "But hurry back, and don't forget where you were."

Lara rose and quickly got them more drinks. Handing an open bottle to her friend she said, "Steve was busy with his music and with his baseball scholarship, and for the first time in three years I had many free hours without him. I wanted to rush for a sorority. I wanted to be popular. And…well, I was really curious. I wanted to know what dating another guy would feel like. I started sneaking out on Steve. I lied to him all the time. It would have been so much better if I had just been honest with him, but I was afraid of hurting him and…" She looked directly at Jan. "God, I hate even saying this out loud. I…I wanted to be popular, and I liked how the other students treated me with respect when they saw me with Philip. He was my 'in' to every dance and party. My roommates all liked Steve, but Phillip had so much charisma and charm that he had them all atwitter too.

"My roommates were making fun of me because I was still a virgin, and although Steve was still the frontrunner in my head, I didn't feel like I could say, 'Heh, I changed my mind, take me to bed, I want to see what it's all about NOW!' So, one rainy Saturday afternoon I found myself alone at my apartment. I called Steve and told him that I had a bad cold and was going to take some cold medicine and have a nap, and then I called Phillip and asked him if he wanted to come over."

Lara paused and watched Jan's reaction, but her friend's expression remained sympathetic.

"I didn't plan on having sex," she explained, "I just thought we could fool around for a while and then he'd go home. Anyway, he came over. He told me he was tired of waiting, that there were plenty of women who would love his attention, and like a total idiot I still wanted him. It wasn't very long before I was letting him touch me in ways Steve had been denied. I couldn't see past the moment."

Jan still said nothing. Lara's hands were shaking so badly that she had to set her beer bottle on the table, and her voice was hushed.

"Philip kept pressuring me further, and things got out of hand. Or, well...I don't know, maybe I had this planned in the back of my mind the whole time. Eventually Philip wore me down and we ended up having sex." She turned clouded eyes on her friend. "I could never bring myself to call what I did with Philip 'making love.' It was crude and horrible, and I got no enjoyment out of any of it past the kissing. When it was over, I knew how stupid I had been, and after Phillip left I cried when I thought of how tender it would have been with Steve."

Lara shut her eyes, trying to keep herself from seeing in her mind any more of the past. "Philip got up from the bed and walked naked toward the bathroom. In the hall...he met Steve. My phone had rung several times during the day, but I never answered. It must have been Steve worrying about me. He pushed past Philip and saw me nude for the first time in his life." She broke into a sob. "As long as I live, I will never forget the look on his face, nor the question he asked me. 'Did he hurt you?'"

Lara couldn't look at her friend, she was so full of shame. She forced herself to continue. "He was so kind and concerned. He thought I'd been raped. In tears, I shook my head. And then he asked his final question. 'Did you agree to this?' At that moment, I knew it could never be the same between us. I had demolished what we'd had. So, I nodded my head, and that's the last time I saw him—until a couple of weeks ago. When I went looking for him at his apartment the next week, I heard that he had dropped out of school, packed his truck and left the next morning."

Lara stared out into the river with damp eyes that saw nothing and everything. Beside her, Jan's voice sounded forced with emotion.

"You were just a kid, Lara. We all make mistakes."

"True," Lara admitted. She'd told herself that a hundred times before. "But some of us pay for a lifetime."

Chapter Seven

Steve watched, entranced, as towering pines danced across the shimmering surface of the water. Their reflection made the river seem hundreds of feet deep, when in reality a person could easily wade through most of it.

He had been in Island Park for three weeks now with little progress on his mission, and he'd promised himself that he would leave the week after the Fourth of July. Today he'd spent cleaning and decorating the lodge for the holiday, and banners and flags adorned every available space. Jan had given him the evening off, warning him that tomorrow would be hectic.

A few yards from his cabin, resting lazily against a gnarled trunk with the river at his feet, Steve let his mind wander back to last Saturday night at the bar. He could still see the pained way Lara had looked at him, and he mentally kicked himself for acting so bitter. Hell, he was thirty-three, old enough to let the past lie. He'd wanted to show her that she didn't mean that much to him, but instead he'd proven that he'd never gotten over her.

Irritated with himself, Steve looked around for a rock to throw into the clear water of the Buffalo. Realizing the grassy bank didn't have many stones, he reached for the closest thing he could find and used it to make loud splashes. From the appearance of the old piece of barn wood, and the woodpile from which it came, it looked like some kids had tried to build a raft to float the river just like Huck Finn. Pieces of nylon rope still held some of the boards together.

Steve was enjoying the way the board made huge rings every time he slapped the water when he heard someone yelling. Startled, he swung his head from side to side and looked around, alert as ever for the danger that he knew was coming for him. But this was the voice of a woman, and he relaxed somewhat, knowing that it wasn't *those* people.

He listened closely but didn't hear anything further, so he guessed that it was just someone calling to a friend. So, just like a kid, he went back to making waves in the Buffalo.

He heard the sound again. It kicked his protective instincts into action, and he started looking around for the genesis of the noise. Maybe someone was hurt or drowning. Maybe he could do something to help.

Upriver, he could just make out something in the water. Shading his eyes, Steve looked closer and recognized a fisherman.

"Do you need some help?" he yelled, cupping his hand to his mouth.

"Yeah. Could you cut the damn racket? You're scaring the fish!"

Lara. He'd recognize that voice anywhere. She was the fisherman.

Steve took a pair of polarized sunglasses from his shirt pocket. Earlier that morning he had purchased them from Jan's store, and the effect when he put them on was startling. His surroundings seemed to burst into life. The greens were greener, the sky bluer, and he could see Lara perfectly where she stood thigh-deep in the river's limpid water.

Her back was to him, and he watched in fascination as she lifted her arm above her head to cast. With a flip of the wrist, her line flew across the surface of the water as graceful as any bird on the wing. Then, with great patience and dexterity, she reeled the fly back toward her, leaving fish to contemplate eating it for supper.

She was dressed in the height of fashion for a fly-fisherman, Steve saw. A multi-pocketed vest held flies, extra line, and even a net. Her neoprene waders resembled a wetsuit a diver might wear, and it fit her like a glove. Lara in *skin-tight* waders… It was almost more than he could bear.

She faced upstream, so Steve watched her unobserved. She looked damn good. His glasses made her long carefree hair look as if King Midas had touched a finger to it, and the dazzling, sparkling, sensuous water lapped at her buttocks in a most erotic way. As she turned to her side, Steve saw how the fullness of her breasts made the fishing vest hang away from her waist in a most feminine fashion.

Lara. She had grown up. She was all-woman now. Fifteen years ago he had thought her grown, but now he saw that he'd been wrong. Of course, his best view of her assets had been the worst day of his life.

He could still remember her sitting up in that bed. A sheet covered her from the waist down, but her budding breasts were there on display. Small and pert, they were smaller than others he'd pondered over in magazines, but he'd loved them anyway because they were a part of Lara. He recalled the way her shiny hair had almost touched the rosy tips…

Oh, how he had wanted her. But she had allowed another man the pleasure he'd expected them to share. He had left her that day, run to his own apartment, packed everything he possessed into his car and left for good. He remembered driving through that October night, and he began to shake as he did. He'd loved her so much. Loved the way she laughed, with her mouth wide open and holding her belly. The way she'd sit next to him in his truck and rest her hand casually on his knee. The way she would sneak up behind him and harmonize in his ear with whatever he was singing. Yes, he'd wanted to desperately to take her to bed and make tender love to her for days on end, but that was just the beginning of what he'd wanted.

He'd driven blindly that night, crying all the way back to L.A. He'd had other desires, such as going back and showing her just how much and how long he had wanted her, regardless of what had just happened, but the urge was too strong and it would have no good end. He'd known he must put a great distance between them before it was too late.

Trembling uncontrollably, he reached for a cigarette and then swore softly when he realized it had been years since he'd given up the habit. There had to be some other method of calming himself down.

A sudden slight movement from the end of Lara's line caught his attention. She had a fish! Steve watched as she pulled the small trout to her net, carefully removed the hook, and released it.

"She's one of the best fly-fisherman in the west."

At the sound of Jan's voice behind him, Steve jumped. He had to get out of this stupid trance. Letting his guard down like that could be fatal. He had men after him. That was the reason he couldn't settle down here. He had to keep moving as soon as this weekend was over. He had to keep moving until he figured out exactly how he would get out of this mess.

"She always talked about fishing," he replied, only half paying attention to his boss, "but when did she become an expert?"

"After her divorce, she moved up here to live with her uncle. She spent every waking hour on the river. She told me that one hour of fishing did her more good than twenty hours of therapy. From what I can gather, Phillip really did a number on her."

Divorce? Steve's heard skipped a beat. "Phillip? That's right. Phillip Barnhart. Wealthy bastard. I read in an L.A. paper that they married, but I never heard about a divorce." He paused and tried to ask the next question as if he really didn't care, but he wasn't sure about his success. "What happened?"

Jan sat down next to him and shook her head. "Don't know. Lara doesn't like to talk about it. I've even asked her Uncle Lawrence, but he doesn't seem to know much either. It must have been pretty bad though. You should have seen her when she moved up here. Dark circles under her eyes like she hadn't slept in months, and she was a bag of bones."

Steve fought down the rage he felt at the thought of Philip or any other man hurting her. *Get a hold of yourself,* he told himself. *She made her own choices. This has nothing to do with you.*

Jan rose to her feet and brushed the grass from her bottom. "Well, speaking of…I think I'll drive up to the TroutHunter and spend a while with Lawrence. We kind of have a thing for each other," she added in a continued spillage of information. "So, see ya in the morning."

As his boss walked away, Steve turned back upstream. He was disappointed to see that Lara had disappeared. But, it was for the best, really. His belly twisted when Jan told him of Lara's divorce, but that feeling was a mistake. He couldn't afford to focus on her, even if she was available. There more important things at the moment, like staying alive.

He read a book on fly-fishing for awhile, and then, trying to shake off thoughts of Lara, he decided to go for a walk before it got too dark. In the growing dusk he listened to the call of the sandhill cranes echoing down the canyon, and a mother blackbird cawed a warning as he drew too near her nest full of babies in a bushy willow. Quiet evenings here could bring peace to even the most stressed of souls.

Across the river, he heard the crunch of dry twigs. He had probably frightened a deer coming to drink. The sounds of nature blended well with the subdued murmur of the river.

With thumbs looped in his pockets, Steve walked along the bank for about a quarter of a mile, gazing at the cozy log cabins lining the river's edge. Some of the structures stood dark and lonely, waiting for families to arrive for the weekend and fill them with love and laughter. Others held the warm glow of lamplight beckoning weary travelers to stop and rest.

His throat burned with the desire to be a part of something, to be a part of someone's life. To be able to come home at night, relax, talk of his day and hers, to laugh and play and dream and love. The life he had chosen had made him an excess of money, had been full of excitement when he needed it, but last month his priorities had changed. He was beginning to think that the fast lane wasn't the best lane. Hell, he had thousands of dollars in a bank in California that he couldn't draw out. Trying to get at it would be suicide. The good news was, he'd certainly learned he could live without any luxuries.

A cabin with a huge deck overlooking the river and the national forest beyond came into view. It was the last house on this side of the water, and the night was getting darker by the minute, so Steve decided to turn around before he couldn't find his way. As he did, the soft strains of a familiar melody made him stop.

The Righteous Brothers hit "You've Lost That Lovin' Feeling" drifted out over the deck. Slowly, Steve turned to look up through the growing darkness at a figure standing there, her hands touching the deck rail, her long and silky hair tumbling over her shoulders.

He hadn't known she lived here, just feet from where he slept each night in his little one-room cabin.

Steve's stomach rumbled, and he blamed it on the deep timbre of Bill Medley's tones. This song had always made Lara so sad. She'd never wanted the band to play it, and she hadn't wanted to sing it. She'd once made Steve promise that they would never feel that way about each other. Oh, young, naïve love.

He heard her gentle voice and had a crazy urge to recite Shakespeare. *Ah, she speaks!* "I'm so sorry, Steve. I was a fool."

He glanced around. It was clear that she spoke to the forest, as she couldn't know he stood below. He didn't make a sound, didn't even dare breathe for fear of disturbing or embarrassing her. But, Lara's sincerity gripped his heart and threatened to rip it from his chest. He shut his eyes against the pain and wanted to shout, *Why?* But he couldn't get a word past the rigid lump cutting off his air.

Stuffing his hands deep into his pockets, Steve waited quietly until she went inside. It took reserves of strength he didn't know he had.

Then he walked slowly home to bed.

* * *

Steve's legs were tangled tightly in his sheets, and his patience snapped as he tried to free himself from the small double bed. He had suffered one hell of a night, and he didn't feel a bit better this morning.

Finally escaping the bed, Steve walked two steps to the fireplace, crumpled up Island Park's weekly newspaper and threw a match in with it. He released a deep sigh, seeing his breath in the cabin. Even in July, the early mornings here were chilly.

As he dressed, he thought of the questions that had plagued him for the last eight hours. He knew without a doubt that he teetered on the edge of a danger zone. He felt like a man falling from a skyscraper, and no matter what he did he couldn't pull himself back. He wanted to fill in the blanks of Lara's life since they separated. Was that her own house on the river, or did she live with her uncle? What kind of music did she like now, and who were her favorite artists? Did she have children? She'd always wanted a child. What did she do when she wasn't fishing? The list went on and on.

Steve raked fingers through his unruly hair and wondered what Lara thought of his new look. Hell, he couldn't even tell her why he had to wear this disguise. But that was the point. It was a disguise, and he needed to stay disguised. As Steve pulled on his cowboy boots with a jerk, he repeatedly told himself that he couldn't get involved, couldn't even *think* about letting himself get involved. And, hell. Even if he were in a situation where he could have a romantic relationship—which he wasn't—he could never allow it to be with Lara. Not ever again.

But…he had changed so much in fifteen years. Why couldn't she have learned a lesson or two along the way, too? They had just been kids. Whatever had happened that day so long ago, it sounded like she regretted her mistake.

In the cabin's tiny bathroom, Steve washed his face, brushed his teeth, and pulled his hair back in a ponytail. He grinned into the mirror, thinking his father would take him to the woodshed if he ever saw his hair like this, but then he sobered. God, he missed his family. He hoped they were all right. He didn't dare take the chance of calling them.

Moved by thoughts of his family, he made a sudden decision. It was foolhardy, perhaps, but he'd be moving on from here soon enough. He wanted to look like himself the next time he saw Lara, didn't want to be wearing the face of another man, a man on the run. A man who should be on the hunt.

He went outside his cabin and confronted his patriotic handiwork of yesterday. Pond's Lodge looked proud of its American heritage. The flags were blowing gently in the breeze, and filled him with pleasure.

Running into the store connected to the bar, he bought a razor and shaving cream from Susan and asked her if she could cut hair.

She stared at him with uncertainty. "No!" she said, shaking her head. "But Jan can. She used to be a beautician."

"Cool," Steve said, and he excitedly headed back to his room.

A half hour later he had a clean-shaven face that was much whiter than his forehead, but it felt great; it was *him*. He put out the fire in the hearth, grabbed a Levi's jacket and stepped into the crisp air and bright sunshine. As he did, he felt a strange sensation of being home. Maybe it was due to the sights and sounds of the nature around him: The scent of pines was always stronger in the morning, a smell fresher than home-baked bread, and the sandhill cranes were kicking up a lively tune.

He found Jan easily enough. She was already sitting at the bar. The tantalizing aroma of coffee led him toward her. She already had her hair-cutting gear set up, which only surprised him a little. Susan, as usual, had wasted no time in relaying all relevant information.

When she looked up from her coffee, she almost spat it out. "My God, where did that face come from?"

He grinned. "My mom and dad. Are you ready to cut some hair?"

"I guess so," she said. "That pony tail looks a little ridiculous now! How short do you want it?"

Steve showed her the length he wanted, and she sat him down on a low bench, wrapped a professional cape around his neck and began by cutting his ponytail clear off. Then she started shaping the rest, leaving the back a little long.

When she was finished, she looked at him with her head tilted to one side. "Wow, you are one handsome sonovabitch!"

Steve laughed and removed the cape. "Thanks, Jan, I feel ten pounds lighter."

"You look ten years younger!"

"How much do I owe you?"

"Are you kidding? This one's on the house. Just let me look at you all day long."

"Uh, so, what *are* the plans for today?" Steve asked, laughing.

"This is our busiest week of the year. Today especially. We won't worry about repairs or anything. I'd just like you to help out in the store, cafe, or bar, wherever you're needed most."

Steve nodded and sipped the hot coffee she handed him.

"You won't have to sing tonight," Jan continued, "because everyone in town will be at the fireworks display at Lakeside Lodge."

Steve glanced at her. "They dare shoot fireworks in such a wooded area?"

Jan nodded. "Lakeside Lodge is on the reservoir overlooking Bill's Island. We have a lighted boat parade at dusk and then the fireworks over the water. That way, the fire department can regulate the crowd and the fireworks. It's a fun, festive, family affair."

"There's *another* lodge around here besides yours and The TroutHunter?" Steve asked in astonishment. "How many are there?" He was embarrassed he hadn't asked for this information beforehand, but he'd been fixated on working, singing, and not thinking about Lara.

"Lakeside is behind us about ten miles. It sits on the shore of Island Park Reservoir. It's a gorgeous location. There's also Sawtelle Mountain Resort, Island Park Village, A River Runs by It, The Pines, and Mack's Inn."

"And there are enough people that come here to fill every one of those places?"

"Sure are," Jan said, sweeping up Steve's thick hair from the floor. "In fact, most of us are already booking for Christmas through March. The snowmobilers come from all over the world to soar along our six-hundred and fifty miles of groomed trails."

"Damn. Do you ever have a down time?"

"Spring," Jan said. "The snow isn't gone, but it's patchy, and the ground is usually too wet to camp, and no wildflowers are out yet. But in the fall we get hunters from all over the U.S., and some international folks even pay fees to hunt here. So spring is when we try to get all remodels and repairs done. And most of us shut down for a week or two to take a short vacation someplace warm."

Steve nodded. He could see that making sense.

"Of course, it's not just tourists that we accommodate. We have around four thousand people who live here year-round, and in the summer that number swells to twenty-five thousand every weekend. There are cabins and huge summer homes all over the woods, and large campgrounds too. When you consider we have a reservoir, Henry's Lake, The Snake River, The Buffalo River and about ten smaller creeks full of fish, there's always space to roam. And the fact that we are only a thirty-minute drive from the west entrance to Yellowstone doesn't hurt either."

Jan looked somber. "I'm afraid I'll be busy today with accidents also. There's a group of volunteer EMTs that handle all calls, and I'm captain of our local fire department. Of course, many of the homes are remote around here, so at drills every week we work on using maps to quickly locate addresses." She grunted. "It's not like a city at all. It's more like a scavenger hunt."

"I bet," Steve said.

She shrugged and looked at him. "We're blessed. We have lots of firefighters and paramedics, EMTs and doctors up here who aren't officially part of the volunteers. If they see an accident or someone sick they'll take over until we can get to them. Thank goodness. Every year we seem to have so many people getting hurt, crashes in vehicles or four-wheelers or boats. So...you'll need to stay close enough to fill in for me if I'm needed elsewhere."

"This place amazes me," Steve said. "And it seems like *you* do it all."

"I like being independent," Jan said. "That's why I love it here. But, no time for any more gabbing, we'd better get rollin'. Why don't you take over at the shop while Susan and I wait tables for a couple of hours? Breakfast should be a booming business this morning."

Chapter Eight

The day was busier than even Jan anticipated.

Swarms of customers flocked in and out of Pond's Lodge. Steve worked in the grocery store until mid-afternoon and then traded Jan places to tend bar. There were a few times in the day that he had to do both when, as predicted, she got an EMT call. A boy was injured in a boating accident, and an hour later they picked up a girl who had crashed on her four-wheeler. Before night fell, Jan and two other EMTs from town had responded to a heart attack, a wound from a chainsaw, and a dog bite.

Jan walked wearily into the bar just after nine p.m. "This last one was a bad one," she muttered. Steve watched her drawn expression as, shaking her head, she continued. "I don't know how Lara does it. She stays so calm and handles the situation just like a doctor."

Steve was surprised. "Is Lara an EMT?"

"Yep, the best. We all certified together a few years ago. We saw too many accidents and had to stand by waiting for someone from Ashton to come thirty miles up the hill. Lara said she'd wanted to train as a nurse when she was younger and thought it would be a great idea to go to classes as a group.

"Anyway, we got a call an hour ago that a baby fell into Elk Creek. Lara beat us there, and we're two miles closer! Apparently she was just passing the turnoff on her way home from work when she heard the call on her scanner. When she arrived, the baby was in the water. Luckily the river is slow-moving there and the little girl hadn't gone downstream, but she was lodged under a bridge and had been without air for at least ninety seconds."

Jan looked up at Steve, and he saw the strain in her eyes.

"Lara was doing CPR on the kid when we arrived. She was really killing herself. Just as I was about to take over, the little girl started breathing. We think she's going to be okay, but we have to wait for the doctors to check her out. The ambulance is taking her to Rexburg right now for that. God, it was scary! She's only two years old and was howling like a coyote…which is a good sign, I guess."

Steve wiped his hands on a towel and thought of Lara. She was probably home now, alone. Jan had told him earlier that Lara owned her cabin and that Lawrence lived closer to the TroutHunter. He wondered if she was badly shaken. Probably, considering she'd had to go through that experience, even if she had saved the child's life.

"If you don't mind, Steve," Jan said suddenly, "I think I'll ride up to the fireworks with Lawrence. The store is locked up, and we closed the restaurant for the night, so you'll just have the bar to watch. We won't be long, and then you can turn in. You must be as tired as I am."

Tired? Restless was the word.

Jan was gone just a little over an hour. Most of the bar patrons went to watch the fireworks, but a few old-timers said they'd rather drink than ooh and ah. They kept Steve occupied with stories from the way "fishin' used to be" in the olden days until Jan returned just as promised and took over the bar.

A handsome older man was with her. He took a seat and stuck out his hand. "You must be Steve. I'm Lara's uncle."

The man's pleasant expression put Steve instantly at ease. "Has Lara told you we were friends a long time ago?" he asked.

"Oh, no," the man said as they shook. "She hasn't said a word. But she's been so quiet lately that I asked Jan what the problem was." He paused. "I remember her talking about you constantly when she came up here for summer vacations as a kid. What ever happened between you two?"

Jan pushed Steve out of the way and slid a drink in front of Lawrence. "Interrogate him some other time, dear. Steve's off to bed."

Steve nodded, gave her a thankful smile and walked out the back door of the bar. He was tired, but he was also keyed up. He thought he'd walk his frustrations off, but somehow he headed in the wrong direction to do that. In the stillness of the night, he was walking toward Lara's.

He hoped she would be there. At the same time, he hoped she would be gone.

As he approached the deck side of her two-story home, Steve looked for any signs of movement on the porch. A soft light filtered through a shaded window. He listened through the silence and heard the faint chords of music within.

He stood in front of the door, frozen. He couldn't just walk in and look at her, but really that's all he wanted to do. He wanted to simply watch her move and talk and fill his head with thoughts of her. But if he knocked on her door, he would have to say something. He couldn't imagine what, not a single thing. Not after their past few encounters.

This is bizarre. I've done scarier things than this, he told himself. *All you have to do is knock.*

Breathing shallowly, Steve finally got up enough nerve. The heavy oak door remained shut, but he heard Lara call, "Who is it?"

"Steve," he managed.

A soft groan sounded, and Steve couldn't tell if it came from the door or her. Light flooded his eyes as she threw the door wide, and then Lara stood facing him in nothing but a white football jersey with a number 10 on the front. She looked more like a perfect 20.

"Come in."

She watched him with an expression of shyness, curiosity and wariness. Her hair was pulled high on her head in a lopsided ponytail. The shirt was completely modest and yet not at all. The length came down to mid-thigh, exposing a span of creamy flesh. He wondered how those silky legs would feel wrapped around his hips.

Lara led him inside then stood staring at him from a tiny alcove. She wore no bra, and the material of her shirt couldn't help but cling to the ripe fullness of her breasts, but she crossed her arms and hid those erect peaks from his open admiration. Above her head Steve could see an open-beamed loft with a huge bed as its focal point. "Danger Zone" wasn't even close to a strong enough term for what he was experiencing in the pit of his stomach. He had never wanted a woman so much in his entire life.

She stared at him for a few more seconds, cocking her head to the left and then the right. "Now, there's the Steve I remember. You look ten years younger with your hair short and a smooth face. Did Jan work her magic on you?"

Steve nodded and grinned.

"I approve," Lara said. Then she blushed. Her dark brown eyes still held a nervous seriousness, but now Steve also saw an electrifying tension. "Come in and sit down. I'll be right back."

He watched her holding on to the rail as she walked up the log staircase, but he finally had to turn away when he could look far enough up her leg to see the lace of her panties. He sat down in a soft chair opposite the couch, knowing he couldn't allow himself the pleasure of sitting next to her. That would be pure idiocy.

The cabin was elegant and very comfortable at the same time. Rich wood gleamed on every wall, and Steve noticed green plants everywhere. It was unquestionably a woman's house, but one where any man could feel right at home.

Hearing a creak on the stairs, Steve looked up and watched Lara come back down. Expecting to see her fully clothed, he was surprised to note that she'd just slipped into a pair of jeans. Her feet were still bare, and her glorious hair, a riot of curls. But the thing that most amazed him was that she hadn't put on a bra.

The thought of her naked breasts beneath that jersey made him throb with suppressed longing. He remembered back to the first time he ever touched her. They had been making out in his dad's car, and as he kissed her he found a cord of muscle in her neck that made her arch her breasts into his chest. She'd moaned, "Touch me," and when he hesitated she took his hand and placed it under her shirt and over her lacy bra. Steve's fingers twitched in remembrance of how her nipple felt straining against that fabric.

Lara sat on the couch and tucked her feet up under her. When she didn't speak, Steve realized he would have to break the uneasy tension.

"Jan tells me you had quite an ordeal today. I thought you might need someone to talk to."

Lara's eyes glistened with moisture, but she didn't cry. "Oh, Steve."

He thought his heart would burst at the manner in which she spoke his name.

"It was so frightening. I was having a flat tire fixed at Elk Creek Gas Station when my beeper went off. I couldn't have been more than thirty seconds away. When I got there, her father was still trying to get to her under that little bridge. I scrambled into a niche he couldn't reach and got her foot. Thank God."

She drew a ragged breath, and Steve was ashamed at himself for being more interested in the way her shirt rose and fell than the story she was telling.

"She was only two years old, and even soaking wet and blue I could tell how beautiful she was. I started CPR immediately. I was so afraid of breaking her ribs, but I knew she'd die if I didn't. Her cries when she started breathing again were the sweetest thing I've ever heard."

Steve listened intently as Lara talked. One lonely tear slid down her cheek. She had such compassion, even for strangers, and it reminded him of the girl he once knew. For the moment he had forgotten his lust, but in its place loomed something far more threatening. He wanted to care for Lara in all the ways he'd been denied since that fateful day in college.

It scared the living hell out of him.

* * *

They talked, and Steve was different. Almost friendly. The conversation was everything Lara had hoped from the moment she saw him walking along the highway.

First they caught up on safe subjects: Steve's parents, friends they'd had in common in high school, Lara's Uncle Lawrence. She answered all of Steve's questions about her job, her home, and her EMT work. She noticed that he steered clear of anything too personal, and that drove her a little nuts. She wanted desperately to know everything about him, but she was still a little afraid that he'd jump to his feet and storm out if she asked the wrong question.

"Can I get you a drink?" she offered.

"Sure," he said. "If you've got a beer, that would be great."

A couple of days earlier she had bought a six-pack, just in case he ever decided to stop by, of the beer that had been his favorite in college. She'd felt silly doing it, as it seemed unlikely there'd be a need, but now she felt even sillier. Steve would know she'd been hoping he'd come.

She walked over and handed him the dark-green bottle. He turned the label toward him.

"Dos Equis? Don't tell me I finally won you over from Corona and bitch beer to the dark side."

Lara laughed and held up a raspberry Bartles and Jaymes. "Sorry," she told him with a grin, "but I'm still a lightweight. I bought those for you."

He sat easily in her comfortable, oversized chair, his elbows raised onto its soft back. Lara couldn't tell if he was happy or mad. One scuffed boot rested on the opposite knee, and each move of his body, each fluctuation of his voice, made a lasting impression on her mind—and other places. Lara couldn't believe how physically attracted she still was to this man.

He wore a white cotton shirt with the sleeves rolled up. His jeans were faded but clean, and they clung seductively to his powerful legs. She felt a tingle move up her arms and through her breasts as she watched him take a long slow sip and then wedge the bottle in between his thighs.

The conversation lulled into an uncomfortable silence. Lara wished he would stay forever. Hearing his soft, deep voice made her feel like he belonged here. Maybe a little closer, even.

"I enjoyed your music the other night," she said. "I thought you were a good singer before, but you've improved."

"Experience, that's the only difference."

"Have you been singing a lot, then?"

Steve shifted in his chair, took another gulp of beer and placed both feet on the floor. Hunched over, he locked his fingers and dangled the bottle between his knees. After another moment of quiet, he looked up and deep into her eyes, and his voice held a heart-wrenching note of sadness when he answered.

"I don't mean *performing* experience. I'm talking about life. The more you live, the more you understand. That's why I sing better now. I've got my own story to bring to the music. My own feelings. My own pain."

Lara tried to remain unmoved, to not beat herself up about the past. This wasn't only about her. Still, her poise felt like the seeds of a dried flower scattered by a mighty wind. And that wind was blowing her toward Steve for the second time in her life.

He stood. "I'd better get going."

Seated, Lara was eye-level with his belt buckle, so she had no choice but to raise her head and look him in the eyes before she embarrassed them both. Jumping to her feet, she walked him toward the door. "Thanks for stopping by, Steve. I really am sorry for—"

He cut her off in mid-sentence. "Let's save that baggage for another time. You've had a traumatic day, and I'm sure you're beat. Let's try to get together for lunch or something. Soon."

They were at the door now, barely inches apart. Lara shoved her hands into the back pockets of her jeans to keep from touching him, but when his eyes fell on her jutting breasts she quickly moved them to her front pockets.

"Goodnight, Lara," he said.

His green eyes captured Lara's imagination. She wanted to see him laugh and cry, but most of all she wanted to see those eyes grow serious with desire. She stood mesmerized, and after a moment Steve lifted a rough finger to her face and ran its coarse tip from her cheek to her chin and back. He didn't speak, and Lara couldn't. Then she watched him open the door and walk down the dark path outside and disappear.

Steve. It had surely taken almost everything out of him to visit her. Swallowing his pride had never been one of his better qualities, but he had made the effort to see her tonight. Lara wondered exactly what that meant.

Heading to bed, she supposed they still had some time to figure that out.

* * *

The baby's lifeless little body lay on the hard ground.

Lara groaned and pumped the child's chest, then blew air into her tiny mouth. She continued for some time when suddenly the chest was no longer that of a toddler. Lara looked up to see the baby smiling in her mother's arms, and other people watching, and she herself smiled at the beautiful picture the pair made. She had saved the baby. All was well.

So, why was there still a body on the ground?

She didn't want to look away from the mother and child, but she knew she was needed elsewhere. In slow motion, her eyes traveled back to the earth. Under her palms lay the chest of a man, dark tufts of hair covering the developed muscle of his pectorals. The sight startled her, but she looked to see if the man was breathing. That's when she saw it was Steve. He lay stone-still.

Frantically, she began compressions. She raised her head to the people standing above, but they had all disappeared. Again and again she compressed Steve's chest and then moved to his mouth to blow life into his motionless body. Her back and neck ached, and her arms went numb, but she continued. Only after what seemed like an eternity did she finally collapse from the strain, and when she did, she fell helplessly on Steve's cold body.

A shrill scream sounded, and Lara raised her head from several pillows. Her own cries had awakened her. It had all been a dreadful, horrible, realistic dream.

She pulled damp hair away from her fevered face and tried to breathe evenly. Although it was just a dream, Lara knew beyond a doubt that it had come as a warning. She'd had dreams like this several times before in her life. She'd had one a few days before her dad passed. She'd had one the night before she had a car accident in high school. The dreams were always predictions.

Steve Mitchell was in imminent danger.

Chapter Nine

It had been three long days since Steve saw Lara.

He'd sworn to himself that he was going to move on, but he hadn't brought himself to tell Jan. He'd tried to submerge himself in his work for her, but even strenuous labor did nothing for his emotional state. Lara was everywhere—her reflected image in the shiny counters he polished, in the amber liquid he poured, and most disturbing, her presence was in every single song he sang.

He didn't know why he was sticking around. He could probably find better information elsewhere about his main task, and Lara hadn't rushed to see him again even though he'd said they should have lunch or something soon. He supposed the distance was for the best, as danger lurked everywhere—or could. He might have chosen not to flee, but that didn't change the fact that men were after him who weren't above hurting anyone close to him or those who got in their way. He couldn't allow Lara to be involved.

Yet, loneliness was driving him nuts. Desire. Loss, damn it! How could he be feeling the loss of someone who'd stepped out his life more than fifteen years before? Was he afraid that she'd already decided to step out of his life again?

He'd been going on walks in his spare time, and with Lara living so close it seemed incredible that he hadn't just bumped into her over the past few days. Jan had mentioned that The TroutHunter had a group of Russian businesspeople visiting Island Park to fish, so maybe she was tied up with that. Logic, however, told Steve that nothing would stop her if she wanted to see him badly enough.

Lifting an ax over his head, Steve split a log into several pieces. Physical labor was the best remedy for an immeasurable hunger. He wouldn't go after her again.

"Steve," Jan called from the side door of Pond's. "Can you come here a minute?"

Steve entered the lodge, letting his eyes adjust to the dark interior. Jan sat at the bar hunched over a mug of beer. She was dressed in her usual attire of jeans and t-shirt. "Did you need me?"

"Our community first-responders are sponsoring a coed softball game and dinner with Ashton's fire department. Would you be willing to play with us on Saturday?"

Steve laughed. "I haven't played ball for years, but I'd be happy to try if you don't mind a little rust."

"We need you, dear," Jan assured him. "You'll do fine."

A good game was just what he needed. It was a throwback to college, really, when he'd played on scholarship, though he'd given that all up when he left school. Steve felt blood start pumping through his veins as if he were already rounding second base and heading to third. Or was it the fact that, as an EMT, Lara would probably be there?

* * *

Lara shut the sliding door of the rented van and waved as her Russian guests left for the airport in Idaho Falls.

It had been an exhausting week. She had dreaded the trip since last December when the businessmen booked it, and she'd studied a Russian dictionary for days before their arrival to learn a few phrases that would help her explain the week's arrangements and the basics of fly-fishing. She needn't have worried. The group leader spoke excellent English, and he relayed every detail to the rest of his men. Not that the language barrier would have been too significant. Fly-fishing was one of the quietest sports in the world. Verbal communication was very rarely necessary.

Surprisingly, she'd found the Russians to be expert fly-fisherman, so expert in fact that she spent her week learning as much from them as they did from her. As well, the enchantment of the valley really got to everyone, and it wasn't long before the group was acting like the place was their home. Lara had never cherished her native land as much as she had in the past few days. She looked at it through fresh eyes. The greens seemed greener, the sky vaster, and the river more majestic than ever before.

Was that because of Steve, though? Thoughts of him had surfaced frequently, like a trout bursting to the top of the water for something to eat. She had avoided him, mostly because she wasn't certain where things could go and she was nervous about the meaning of her dream. She had been extremely busy, too, but nothing in this world or any other kept her from recalling the sound of his raspy voice and the sensation of his coarse fingertip as it gently brushed her cheek. Sometimes, when the wind rose unexpectedly on the river, Lara could almost feel his touch. When that happened, shivers of anticipation pervaded her being.

She'd hoped her time away would get her head on straight, but it hadn't. Each night, as she lay in her cozy bed in her loft, Lara gave in to the luxury of fantasy. She hadn't been with anyone since her divorce. She'd been on a few dates that had ended up very platonic. Thinking about Steve now, her body as well as her mind surrendered to the idea of reclaiming everything she'd lost. However, when the stark light of dawn forced her back to reality, Lara understood only too well that her illusions were just that. She would be foolish to imagine the two of them could rekindle anything after the way she'd betrayed him.

With her guests gone and her uncle running the store, a lonely Friday night stretched out before her. She considered stopping at Pond's for a drink, but her distressed appearance made her change her mind. A windy day in Box Canyon had destroyed her head of curls, and her face resembled a raccoon's where the sun had burned her cheeks around her sunglasses. She had the big softball game tomorrow, so she should go home, soak in a tub for an hour and then get to bed early, but she didn't want to get to bed early—at least not alone. And Steve had mentioned getting together for a meal....

Where in God's green earth had *that* thought come from? Lara shivered, an acute shudder of embarrassment. Steve would never allow her to get that close. He'd been burned once, and with him a person only got one shot. At least, that's how he'd been in the past. She'd screwed up her chance fifteen years ago, and the most they would ever do was talk about the mistake she'd made. Not that she wanted to do that, really.

Unlocking the front door of her cabin, Lara threw her keys on the couch and walked to the bathroom. A hot, steamy bath there relaxed knotted muscles, but it did nothing for the tightness in her stomach.

She spent an hour plucking her eyebrows, shaving her legs, painting her toenails and conditioning her hair; then, wrapped in a lightweight robe, Lara stepped onto her deck.

The faint chords of a guitar filtered up the river through the twilight, and Lara quickly turned around and went inside. In spite of her resolve to stay home and finish the novel she had been reading for the last couple of weeks, she found herself dressing in a soft denim tiered skirt, her turquoise-and-brown cowboy boots and a tank top to match, and before long her feet were moving of their own accord along a path at the water's edge. Knowing what she should do and actually doing it had always been a problem for Lara. She occasionally let her heart rule her head, and this seemed to be one of those times.

She soon found herself on the front porch of Pond's Lodge with a shaky hand on the doorknob. Her first experience with Steve in this bar had been a disaster; her second, the same. True, they had made some headway since then, but she had no idea where she stood now. Her confidence waned as she remembered his angry glares.

Lara backed away from the door as a group of laughing friends approached from the parking lot. "Coming in?" a man asked, offering Lara a kind smile.

"Not now," she said, shaking her head. She couldn't. She couldn't walk in there, sit down, have a drink and act as if Steve were a mere acquaintance. Not tonight. Steve would read her stark need for him in her eyes, and things would get heavy.

Jan had purchased heavy wooden play equipment, complete with swings and slide, for the children who spent their vacations at the lodge, so Lara wandered across the parking lot and sat down on a swing. She could hear every word Steve sang from here, every little inflection in his gravelly voice. She let the rhythm of the music and the motion of the swing lull her into a dream world. She could shut her eyes and imagine the movements of his lips as he sang or the sudden flash of white teeth when he gave the crowd a smile.

Sometimes she felt jealous of his guitar. He always held it so close to his chest, strumming and stroking it, making it sing with his touch.

She listened to him sing but detected an underlying struggle in the familiar songs. When he sang about being "All out of love," she wanted to rush into the lodge and prove him wrong. But he sounded so sincere, so sure of himself, that she didn't even stand up. Once again she recognized a new depth of emotion in Steve, and she pondered the reasons. Was it all about her, or had there been other difficulties in his life? He'd had to have known other women. He'd *had* to.

Lara was so consumed by her thoughts that she didn't hear the music stop. At first she didn't see Steve standing on the porch, either. He'd walked outside for some fresh air during his break.

Lara silently stopped the movement of her swing, sitting completely still in the darkness. She knew he hadn't seen her, and yet she honestly didn't want him to know she was there.

He walked within a few feet as he migrated toward the bank of the river and then gazed up the waterway toward her cabin. At first she thought he'd noticed her, but the unexpected deep timbre of his voice startled her and his words changed her mind.

"Where are you, Lara Douglas? And would you please get out of my head?"

Steve turned slowly and walked back inside. Lara sat dead still, and she remained that way until long after he'd left.

He was thinking of her. She was "in his head."

The thought invigorated her more than any other high she'd ever experienced.

Chapter Ten

Lara watched Steve warm up from the confines of her jeep. His dark hair curled slightly at his neck from the back of his baseball cap, ample shoulders rippled under his thin t-shirt, and his butt looked tight and firm under the worn jeans. Lara would have given him anything he wanted at that instant—anything, and he didn't even know it.

She sat for a full five minutes in her jeep, her hands draped loosely over the steering wheel, watching, just watching, the bulge of his upper arm as he threw a softball to another man. She also watched two female firefighters from the opposing team flirt outrageously with him. Dixie bent over slowly in front of Steve and made sure he saw her perfect ass as she picked up a ball she'd missed on purpose, and Angie scooped up a softball one-fourth the volume of her oversized plastic breasts, pulled her shirt tighter for Steve, and gave her signature giggle.

Still, Lara wanted to stay here and observe him for hours. She found herself squinting into the sun just as he did each time he turned to catch the ball. She loved the way he rested his mitt on his hip when someone stopped to talk to him.

"Lara!" Jan yelled from a rickety, bleached bench. "We're ready to start, come on!"

Grabbing her mitt, Lara jumped from the jeep and walked toward her team. They played their games next to the Forest Service station on a flat piece of ground covered in powdery dirt. The field couldn't possibly be described as a diamond. Their makeshift backstop leaned precariously to one side, and if a person got a real good hit the ball was usually lost for good in the lodge-pole pine forest surrounding the field. But everyone always had a great deal of fun at these outings.

Damn, Lara thought. She'd missed her chance to warm up because she'd spent the last few minutes watching Steve—but she planned to do a lot more of that throughout the game.

* * *

Amidst the tangy smell of leather and earth, Steve inhaled the natural essence of pines and another fragrance of a purely feminine quality.

Steve kept his head turned away, but he felt Lara's presence. She plopped herself down next to him, and the scent grew stronger. It was familiar and delicious, and it wasn't just her perfume. He would remember her scent until the day he died. It seemed to be a combination of her hair product, her cologne, and her simple pheromones. If a man could bottle that smell he would be the richest man anywhere. Hell, if a man could simply smell that smell every day of his life he would be the luckiest man in the world.

Seeing the other team take the field, Steve decided it would be wise to reserve his sensuous thoughts for a later time.

"Hey, Lara," he said. "Are you ready?"

"Ready for anything you are."

Her hazel eyes were very green today. It seemed they held the color of the forest in them, and they twinkled with mischief. She was obviously flirting with him.

So much for keeping things light. Still, a relaxed banter would be easier to handle than the earlier conversations they'd exchanged. Maybe it was good they hadn't met up for lunch. A day of fun would let him spend some time with Lara without complicating anything.

He studied her appearance. She wore jeans and the same royal blue t-shirt the rest of the team had, with their EMT emblem over the left breast. But no one else looked as sexy as Lara. The color was great with her dark hair, which she'd pulled away from her face in a tight ponytail then slipped through the hole in the back of her pink camouflage ball cap, which said TroutHunter across the front.

Jan stood in front of the team as they all sat on an old wobbly bench. "Lara, you're up first."

Lara stood, grabbed a bat and stepped a few feet away to take a few practice swings. Jan continued to read the batting order.

"Steve, you'll be our cleanup hitter, batting fourth."

Steve made a small protest. He hadn't played much ball since college, and he didn't know how good anyone else here was. He didn't care to make a fool out of himself, especially in front of Lara, who'd always been a good athlete. Was Jan expecting him to not only play well but be something of a ringer?

Lara stepped up to home plate. Steve watched as she said something to the umpire, who was her Uncle Lawrence, whom Jan had apparently enlisted. Then Lara turned her face to the pitcher and took a sturdy batter's stance. Which was torture. From Steve's angle he had a perfect view of her little rear as she wiggled it from side to side while grinding her feet into the dirt.

A man from the other team whistled and yelled, "Swing that tush, honey."

Everyone around him laughed but Steve. Steve had a strong urge to swing a bat at the side of the man's head.

Lara let the first pitch go by.

"Strike one!" Lawrence shouted.

Lara turned a look of sheer disbelief on him.

"It dropped right over the plate," he explained.

Without a word, Lara turned back to the pitcher and did her little ritual again.

A stab of heat billowed through Steve's belly. He shut his eyes tightly and willed his desire to stay away from other regions of his anatomy. He didn't want everyone thinking that softball did *that* much for him!

A *ping!* from a metal bat brought Steve back to earth. The softball was sailing to deep right field, and Lara was rounding second. As she turned for third, Steve lost the will to breathe. Wisps of her hair had come loose, her arms were bunched at her sides as she ran, and her firm breasts bounced deliciously. This time, Steve had no will to stop the blood in his body from surging where it would.

He was entirely captivated. Nothing, damn it, had changed in fifteen years. Nothing. She'd made him feel this way a million times in his youth, and the feeling was only stronger today.

Lara's stand-up triple was a great start. The next two batters both got on base with walks, which was rare for slow-pitch. Steve wondered if Lara was having the same disturbing effect on the pitcher from Ashton as she was with him. He couldn't see how the man could avoid it.

Steve walked to the plate and with a knot in his gut looked around at the loaded bases. Crazily, he felt just like he was playing little league again when he was eight. Ugh. Two away, down by two, bases loaded, championship game.... He'd choked. In his mind he could still hear that loud-mouthed umpire yell, "Strike three! You're outta here!" No had one spoken to him as he walked back to the dugout that long-ago summer day. Later, the coach took everyone out for milkshakes, but Steve had just gotten on his bike and ridden home. Nobody had come after him.

Well, he'd gone on to earn a baseball scholarship, hadn't he? It was foolish to fixate on past failures. It was foolish to remember the pain and embarrassment and get caught up the long-ago days and—

He stood at the plate, bases loaded, his bat resting on his shoulder, and looked at the crowd. They were eyeing him just as they had that day when he was eight, and he had yet to step into the batter's box.

"Steve!"

He heard Lara's calm voice from third base. It held an almost motherly quality, and he knew she'd realized what he was thinking. She knew about that day, was one of the only people he'd told, and she'd relived it with him often over their years together. Long ago, she'd been his rock. She'd been his biggest fan at the games in high school and college. She'd been a big reason he even tried to get a scholarship for athletics, why he believed in himself enough to keep playing.

She didn't speak again, just raised her right hand and gave him the thumbs-up sign. That had once been their private symbol meaning, *"You can do this. I love you."*

He slammed the first pitch into the forest.

The rest of the game was an exercise in willpower for Steve. He could not for the life of him get his mind off of Lara. He scrutinized her with a voracious lust. Every move she made turned him on. Every word she uttered had the same effect. Hell, every word *anybody* said had him thinking about sex. Words like *slide, slam,* and *score* shot through his body and burst like rockets.

He wanted her. God, he wanted her. But it would be sheer stupidity to give in—for her life, for his life, for his self-respect. He didn't want to be her second choice. He wanted to go back fifteen years and be her first choice, her one and only. Not to mention the fact that his current situation was utterly impossible.

He thought back and cursed his youthful integrity. Why had he been so stupid? Lara had told him she wanted to wait until they were married to make love, and he'd believed her even after their relationship became more intimate and she sometimes told him she didn't want to wait anymore. He'd craved her desperately, but he'd truly believed he was doing the right thing in order to keep her respect. He'd wanted her for a lifetime and beyond.

Lawrence announced the game was over, and relief filled Steve. He just wanted to get away for a while, away from Lara to have a nice cold shower and sleep away this madness.

Jan suddenly yelled above the noise. "Listen up, everybody! Dinner is going to take a little work from everyone. The more you help, the faster we'll eat. Ashton!" she called, addressing the opposing team. "Since you lost the game this year, it's your job to peel the potatoes and set the tables. Our group will prepare the chicken and the cobbler and get the fires going for the Dutch ovens. Supper will be outside, in front of the lodge. Any questions?"

Lara had moved up next to Steve, and with a smile she whispered, "Would anybody dare argue?" Then, "Do you want a ride?"

"Oh, babe," he groaned, using his old pet name for her. "You have *no* idea what you're asking."

She didn't comment, but her impish grin said he might be wrong.

* * *

Every female in the valley had her attention on Steve, and Lara didn't like it. She'd meant to sit by him at dinner, but women already surrounded him at the picnic table by the time she got her food. It was suddenly clear that she was not only up against Steve's old hang-ups; she was also going to have to deal with competition.

The chatter quieted somewhat as everyone filled their empty stomachs, but the babble rose again when their hunger was appeased. Lara rose to help clear the tables. As she did, she noticed Steve's eyes on her, and she couldn't believe the sense of yearning that filled her being. The day had been wonderful and disconcerting at the same time. She loved being near him, and yet his presence reminded her of all the mistakes she'd made. Of how he could probably never completely forgive her.

Her desire for him had been a force all day as she watched him. No detail had been small enough to go unnoticed: the way he rolled his eyes when he made an error, the way he wore his hat a little too far down on his forehead, the times he yelled encouragement to her, and the times he forgot himself for a minute and called her "babe," just like the last fifteen years had never happened. Did the last mean something? Anything at all?

She worked her way to his side of the table and leaned over his shoulder to retrieve his plate. "Are you through?" she asked.

"With what?"

Those green eyes almost knocked her out. She wanted to crawl in and hibernate in their depths.

With me? she wanted to ask out loud, but it was a dangerous question. What if he said yes? She couldn't bear it.

"Are you through with your meal?" she said.

"Yes, thank you."

His reserves were up. He was too polite. But Lara had an urge she couldn't subdue. She moved up close behind him and, reaching for his silverware, delicately brushed her breast against his arm. The women's movement wouldn't approve of such a tactic, but she didn't care. She wanted Steve, and she intended to get him and then keep him for the rest of her life...or go down in flames trying.

She saw Steve bite the inside of his cheek at the contact. That was a start.

A half-hour later, the chores surrounding dinner were completed and the group migrated toward the big bonfire that had been built outside Pond's Lodge. Someone suggested Steve do a little singing. He refused good-naturedly, but as evening fell Jan had his guitar in his arms and he began strumming a lazy cowboy song.

"Don't you know anything with a little more spark?" asked a lady near the fire. "I'm falling asleep."

"Give me some suggestions," Steve said.

"How about an old Beatles tune?" someone called from the dark.

"Okay," he agreed, "some old Beatles songs. But on one condition."

Everyone went quiet, waiting.

"That Lara sing with me."

All eyes turned to Lara; some with curiosity, others with jealousy—like Dixie and Angie—and still a few more with surprise. Quiet rumblings began about her ability to sing. They'd never heard her, ever. Did she have any talent?

Suddenly, the crowd started to clap. Steve grinned at Lara, so without another word she walked to the empty chair he indicated and sat down. She wasn't afraid. They would sound great together. He didn't even have to tell her what song he'd choose; the intro would be enough.

He launched into "Please, Love Me Do"—a steamy and sexy rendition—and within seconds Lara joined in. They shared the mic, and Lara was pleased that her alto voice remained the perfect harmony for his warm baritone. She could also tell from the crowd's glances that she wasn't the only one who sensed the sexual tension dancing between them.

After the first couple of songs, dancing began in the gravel parking lot. Steve and Lara couldn't stop. They sang for over an hour, finally ending with a rousing rendition of "Eight Days a Week."

Lara's ardor for Steve grew with each song. There were times that she felt sure he was singing just to her, and other times he gave the impression he was simply an artist performing as part of a job. Lara was not ready for the latter to be true. Neither was she willing to let this be the end of their night together. She wanted more.

She got sucked into a conversation with a couple of friends. Slowly the crowd began breaking up for the evening, and Lara noticed Steve making his escape. She quickly thanked Jan, told her uncle goodnight, and rushed after Steve's darkening figure. He was walking toward his cabin behind the lodge.

"Steve," she called after him. He hesitated but kept walking. She hurried after him.

"Steve, it's really quite dark out here tonight. Would you mind walking me home?"

"What about your jeep?" he asked.

"Uncle Lawrence needed it," she lied.

By now they had reached his cabin door, and he stopped and looked down at her. His face was mere inches from hers.

"Lara," he said, "I know what you're trying to do here, and I'm not playing that game—although the thought of getting you naked has crossed my mind over a thousand times today. We're not the kids we once were. But I'm sweaty from the game, and we've still got some serious shit to discuss before..." He shook his head then gently kissed her on the forehead before turning away to unlock his cabin door. "I'm just going to say goodnight. You're a big girl, you know your way home in the dark without any protection from me."

"Will you go on a picnic with me tomorrow?" Lara asked.

Steve turned back around. He seemed to be fighting with himself. Finally he said, "I will if Jan can get along without me for awhile. And if you promise to open up about a few things."

She'd tell him anything and everything. Whatever he wanted to know in order to get her another chance.

"Steve," she whispered, stepping closer to him in the dim light. "I loved singing with you again. We haven't lost our chemistry, have we?"

He took in a ragged breath then sighed. "No, Lara, we haven't. But I'm not so sure that's a good thing."

Without another word or touch, Steve stepped into his cabin and shut the door behind him.

Chapter Eleven

The next morning dawned calm and clear, and Lara scurried around her home like a squirrel gathering her winter supply of nuts. She'd spent her pent-up energy last night making a list of the supplies she would need, and now she rounded them up, preparing the food and getting everything ready to go by ten o'clock in the morning. Then she ran to her garage and pulled a picnic basket lined with red and white checked cotton down from the shelf.

She took extra care with her shower and tried to make her makeup look as absent as possible. The next hour she spent trying to style her hair in ten different ways, but ended up braiding one thick strand down her left side and leaving the rest sleek and flowing. She remembered Steve had long ago liked it best "simply rippling over her shoulders and down her back."

At the break of dawn she'd called Jan and asked if she could steal Steve away for a long lunch, and Jan had joyously consented. Lara also asked her friend to tell Steve she'd pick him up at noon, so he wouldn't have a chance to tell her he'd changed his mind or had too much to do.

Her clothes were laid out on the bed, and she looked at them now, wondering if her intentions would be too obvious.

"Ah, to hell with it," she decided. She didn't give a damn that he knew she was making a play for him. He'd assumed that much last night, and she owed him a little straightforward honesty anyway.

She slid into matching pink panties and bra then slipped a light cotton dress over her head to settle sleekly over her curves. The filmy summer frock looked as if it could have been made in the fifties, but she'd purchased it on her last trip to Idaho Falls. She loved the way the fabric clung to her breasts and bloomed slightly at the waist, and Jan had said it suited her as well. Easing her feet into a pair of black strappy sandals, Lara completed the outfit with silver loops for her ears and a silver ring for her third finger.

She turned and looked in her full-length mirror, and she was pleased to see the melon-colored dress brightened her skin and gave her complexion a healthy glow. Last but not least she sprayed touches of her signature scent on her wrists, behind her ears, and a touch at the shadow of her cleavage.

Loading a blanket and pillows into the back of her jeep, alongside the basket of food and drinks, Lara drove carefully over the gravel road to Steve's cabin. She had it planned in her mind that he would come rushing out to meet her, but after waiting a few seconds she jumped down and went to knock on his door.

There was no answer.

"Steve," she called. "Hello, are you here?"

Still no answer.

Lara turned to Pond's Lodge. Entering through the back side door, she waited a few seconds for her eyes to adjust from the brilliant sunlight outside. Seeing Steve behind the bar pouring a beer for a local construction worker, she felt exceptionally foolish in her dress, especially because Jeb, the construction worker, would most certainly say something.

She tried to get Steve's attention, but he didn't seem to see her. So she cleared her throat.

Way to go, girlfriend, she chided herself. There was nothing sexier than a doing that feminine thing of clearing your throat to get a guy's attention.

Steve and Jeb turned at the same time, and just as she'd expected Jeb let out a slow whistle.

"Good God, woman," he said. "You're apt to give a guy a heart attack comin' in here lookin' like that. Did someone die that I didn't hear about? Or is someone gettin' hung from the marryin' tree?"

"Neither, Jeb. I'm headed to Idaho Falls for my day off, and I felt like looking like a girl for a change. Is that okay with you?" she added tartly.

"Hell, yeah. It's always fine with me, but you have to admit that we rarely see a girly-girl around here."

"Well, Jeb," Lara stated with a twirl. "Take a good look, because you probably won't be seeing one again for awhile."

She turned to Steve after the heat left her cheeks a little. "Is Jan here?"

He shook his head as if coming out of a stupor. "Yeah, she's here somewhere. I'll go find her."

"Hey...!" Jeb shouted as Steve slid into the bar's back room. "Steve? Is that guy's name Steve?" he asked Lara, offering her a questioning look. "I was just tellin' him that two guys were askin' our crew if they'd seen a long-haired and bearded hippie who goes by the name of Steve. He said he didn't know of one."

Lara just stared at Jeb, not sure what to say.

The construction worker took another long drag of beer. "Gonna be one of the hottest days of the year today, weatherman says. That's why I'm hydratin' so early. I'm on afternoon shift this week, and you wouldn't believe how goddamn hot the blacktop can get. Nearly melts your boots to the road."

Again, Lara said nothing.

Jeb took another big gulp, a last one, and stood up. "Well, Lara, you and Jan have a mighty fine time in the Falls today, and think of me when you're in those big expensive shoppin' malls with air-conditioning so all the pretty people don't sweat. You sure do look good, little lady. Sure do."

"Thanks, Jeb," she finally managed. "Have a good one."

He walked over to the exit and left. Just as the door closed behind him, Jan stepped out from the back room. "Is the coast clear?" she whispered.

"Yes, were you hiding from him?" Lara asked.

"Hell, yes! That old goat has been trying to woo me away from your uncle for almost a year now. He's too damn stupid and hard-headed to learn the word no!" She laughed. "You and Steve better get on your way before my lunch crowd comes in. He told me to tell you he'll be waiting in the jeep."

Thinking of Jeb's words, Lara wanted to ask Jan if she'd heard anyone asking for Steve, but she decided against it. Once she got away from the lodge, she could ask Steve what this might be about.

She went back to her jeep, trying to walk as if these were the kind of clothes she wore every day. Steve sat slumped comfortably in the passenger seat, his arm draped casually across the driver's, and as she arrived he mimicked Jeb perfectly.

"Good God, woman, you're apt to give a man a heart attack lookin' like that!"

Lara buckled her seatbelt and gave him a swift backhand to the chest.

They traveled along the gravel road behind Pond's Lodge, and Steve seemed intent on the landscape. Lara would have preferred his undivided attention, but she decided to be patient. At least she'd talked him into coming, if only for an hour or two.

"This day seems so perfect," Steve commented, looking up at the brilliant blue sky. Lara had taken the cloth top off her jeep, and from their seats the landscape was a beautiful blur. "It's hard to imagine that it might be raining by tonight."

"That's just how Island Park is," Lara told him as she rounded a corner. "I've never lived in a place that has such rapid weather changes. One minute it will look like this, and then minutes later we could be drenched to the bone. An hour later it can be sunny again. I guess that's why everything stays so green."

She turned down a muddy lane, driving slowly so as not to splash mud up and onto them. Cottonwood trees made a natural shelter over their heads, momentarily blocking the sun.

"Are we directly behind the lodge?" Steve asked.

"No," Lara said. "We've veered to the right somewhat, why?"

"Just curious. So, if a person was walking, he could go through those pines and end up here? I've kind of lost my directions with all these trees. I've never been back this far."

"Yes," she said, "he could end up here if he knew the way."

Suddenly, an enormous waterway came into view, and they parked the jeep on the edge. It was Island Park Reservoir. The tide of the lake had receded about five feet, and there was a sandy length of beach secluded from everything else.

"Wow! I never would have believed this is just a mile off the main highway," Steve said. "This reservoir is huge. How did you ever find this secluded spot, too?"

"Accidently. It was one summer when I was visiting my uncle. I never told anyone about it, but every chance I got I would slip away to come here and dream."

"What did you dream about?" Steve asked as she laid out a denim quilt with red yarn ties and set her wicker picnic basket upon it. He lay down on the far edge of the blanket, his long length still overlapping the corners. Resting his head in his hand, he looked at her as if waiting for an answer.

For a split second Lara couldn't remember the question. She was bewitched by his elongated physique. How many times had she fantasized about this very moment? All those adolescent years when she'd come here alone, she'd pretended she was with Steve. Now that she really had him here, she wanted very badly to make love with him.

But, no. She needed to stay focused. He had told her that he needed some answers, and she wanted some answers herself.

"What was your question?" she asked.

"What did you dream about as a girl?"

"Lots of things. You know. Just the stuff girls dream about."

"No, I don't know." He stared at her. "Tell me, Lara, what *do* girls dream about?"

She didn't want to divulge her youthful imaginings. How embarrassing, that she'd fantasized she'd be sunbathing and Steve would sneak up on her and make passionate love to her over and over again! But she admitted with a laugh, "Well, now that I think about it, my fantasies haven't changed that much at all."

He gave her an odd, penetrating look, so she changed the subject.

"During the summers when my dad and I visited my uncle I used to ride my four-wheeler here on the back roads every day. I wrote all of my letters to you from right here." She looked out across the Kelly green water and beyond to the dark row of pines that bordered Bill's Island in the middle of the reservoir.

Steve's gaze followed hers. "Did you bring Philip here?"

The mention of her ex-husband's name coming from Steve's mouth startled her. "No, you're my very first."

"I think you're wrong." He laid his head back on the blanket and shut his eyes. "I was *supposed* to be your first—your very first and only, for that matter—but you changed the rules of the game and forgot to tell me about it."

After all this time, it was finally Steve who'd brought up the subject of their past. So there would never be a better time to tell him what he needed to hear and what she desperately needed to say.

"I've analyzed the hell out of what I did," she began, "but even after all this time I can't really tell you why I did that. I guess my head was turned by popularity—and I was naive. I wanted to be accepted and admired. I know that sounds juvenile, but I had a lot of growing up to do."

She removed her sandals and buried her feet in the warm sand of the beach, yearning to touch him while she talked. She'd always imagined that if she ever got the chance to apologize it would be in his arms, but she soon realized how wrong that would be. She needed to give her explanation and let him feel whatever he needed to feel. So she gathered her courage and decided to be as honest as possible. She'd tell him everything.

"Having sex with Philip was a terrifying experience." Feeling cold, she pulled up her knees and drew her full skirt to her ankles. Steve snorted, but she ignored him and continued while she still had the courage. "My friends told me it was never good for the girl the first time, and that I would learn to like it. Somehow, even as inexperienced as I was, I knew that it would have been different with you."

Steve said nothing. Lara supposed there was nothing to say.

She continued. "Afterward, I couldn't get the hurt look on your face out of my head. I refused to see Phillip again, but it didn't matter. When I found out that you'd quit school I knew we were done for good. I felt so alone. I had lost my best friend. I had nightmares for months after you left. I would see the look on your face when you found us...." Her voice broke. "God, Steve, I'm so sorry. I know you were only waiting until I was ready, and then I ruined it for both of us."

"Well, the sex must have gotten better with Phillip—much better," Steve growled. "You married the bastard."

Lara stared at the ground. "After you left, yes, I dated Phillip, but I refused to have sex with him again. Now that I look back on it, he must have seen that as a challenge. He was always very competitive. He wouldn't leave me alone, and I wouldn't give in. Then he suddenly proposed, and everyone told me I would be crazy not to marry him. His family had tons of money, and he had a promising career waiting when he finished law school. I didn't like a lot of the things he did, but I thought that once we were settled and he was away from the frat boys he would calm down."

She took a bottle of water from the picnic basket and took a few sips, trying to calm her nerves. "You have to remember my upbringing, Steve. My parents' religion looks down on girls who aren't virgins when they marry, which I suddenly was. I know you didn't ever quite understand, and to be honest, now I see why, but at the time I believed I was damaged goods. Now I see what a warped sense of thinking that was—and still is, for millions of girls from a number of religions—but in the world I lived in, I could only see what I had always been told. As crazy as it seems…well, I didn't feel worthy of being happy."

Steve shook his head and looked at the ground.

"Phillip was of the same faith, and so that was another reason it made sense that we should marry, two sinners who had helped each sin. He insisted it was the only way to remedy our situation. I was twenty years old, and I'd always followed our faith blindly. Like a lamb to the slaughter, I walked right into a terrible marriage." Lara pulled her knees closer to her chest and hugged herself for comfort. How could she make Steve understand without giving him sickening images that she was still trying to forget? She settled for, "We had only been married three months when I knew I had made a horrible mistake. The sex was dreadful. I have never felt so degraded in my life."

She wanted to see the expression on Steve's face, but she couldn't summon the courage to look at him. She just forced herself to continue speaking. "One night, after having sex, Phillip said something about having a baby. I was shocked and scared. First of all, I knew I didn't want Phillip to be anyone's father. Secondly, Phillip was an only child and he had never once mentioned wanting children. I'd always assumed he'd prefer his rock star–lifestyle to a car seat. Thirdly, and most terrifyingly, I didn't think I was capable of getting pregnant. I'd had five endometriosis surgeries in my teen and college years, and after the last one my doctor told me my chances of conceiving were next to none.

"When I told Phillip, he flew into a rage. I hadn't thought him capable of such horror. He called me every name in the book and then slapped me over and over again, telling me that I had tricked him into marriage knowing all the while that I couldn't have his child."

Lara felt a light touch on her shoulder. It was Steve, but she moved away from him. She couldn't stop talking now; she had to finish, and the worst was yet to come. She had never told anyone this much, but it was time. She'd say it all out loud. Then perhaps she could put it away forever.

Her voice shook with agony. "He told me I had to be the stupidest bitch he'd ever known. Didn't I know why he chose to marry me? He needed a weak little mouse to bear him a kid or two and stay out of his way. He needed a trophy wife, a naïve dense one. One that would never open her mouth to complain or want more than he deigned to share. He required a family to maintain his standing in the church, which had a lot of wealthy people whose business he intended to acquire for his law firm. And, well…he needed a front. Hadn't I seen the way he looked at other guys? Wasn't I even curious as to what or whom he was eyeing in the middle of the night in his locked den?"

Was Steve shocked? Lara turned her head swiftly, her eyes brimming with unshed tears. He wasn't, and he held her stare. So she continued.

"The next week he had me checked into a hospital where the best fertility doctors did every test possible. When they were through, they all came to the same conclusion about my chances: one in a thousand. That night Phillip moved his clothes into the guest room, and he never bothered me again. Of course, within a week he started consistently staying out all night. Then he started getting really bold, and he invited a stranger into our home. A man he'd met in a bar. I stayed awake that whole night listening to my husband having sordid sex with someone else in the next room. I left the following morning."

There. It was finished. She had told him the basic story. She would never discuss the precise humiliation she still felt; nor could she detail the self-esteem she'd forfeited on Philip's behalf. Steve would have to fill in the blanks if he was interested in that.

"I've wanted to apologize to you for so many years, Steve," she finished. "I understand it will never be enough, but at least now you know I paid for it. You were my best friend. That's why it was so important for me to say the words, and I'll always love you for it. *I'm sorry.* And I'll always regret having thrown away your love in return."

Steve said nothing. He simply stared across the water. Really, though, what could he say? Lara didn't expect him to tell her everything about the years they'd been apart, and it wasn't like they could just go back to the way it was. They were both different people now. They had taken different paths, the rules of the game had changed dramatically, and she didn't have a rulebook.

Because she didn't know what to say or do next, Lara begun to mechanically set out the picnic she'd prepared. "I hope you like turkey sandwiches," she said. "I brought a bottle of wine, too, but if you're going to work this afternoon maybe you would rather have soda."

"I'll take the wine," he said. "I could use a drink, and I know you need one—or ten! God, Lara."

She waited for him to say more, but he just uncorked the wine while she got out two goblets.

He poured them each a half a glass of Merlot, took a sip and then touched her shoulder again. This time, she didn't pull away. He wrapped his free arm protectively around her and let her weep.

Afterward, they ate their lunch in silence. Lara picked at her sandwich, but Steve ate ravenously, as if it were his last meal. The disturbing story about her former life didn't seem to have had much effect on his appetite.

"Is there a boat dock near here?" he asked, picking up a second sandwich.

"Yes." Lara nodded over her left shoulder. "It's not far from here. We can drive by it on the way back. Jan keeps a little fishing boat there."

Steve looked interested. "I'd like to do that if you don't mind." He glanced at his watch and then the sky. "Could we go now?"

Lara noticed a few grayish clouds beginning to collect in the distance, and she felt a stab of disappointment. The day hadn't turned out the way she'd hoped. And yet, she had been able to explain her past to him. She'd just…craved something more.

With a deep sigh, she loaded the picnic basket. Steve folded the blanket. Suddenly, he stopped folding and walked over to her. Putting his hand on her shoulder, he looked into her eyes and said, "Lara. I know you wanted more from me today, but I need to sort my thoughts before I can talk about all the things you've said. I've grown up too, and I've seen things that I wish I hadn't. I've also learned that saying the first thing that comes into your head isn't always the smartest idea. Give me a little time."

She nodded, knowing he was being extremely fair.

"Believe me," he continued, his hands moving to her upper arms and gently squeezing them for reassurance, "I heard every word you said. Thank you for being so open. I hope that I can return the favor and share with you some of the ghosts from my past soon, but I've got a few things to tidy up first."

"Can I help?" she asked. She'd do just about anything for him.

A slow smile spread across his face, and for a few seconds, as they made their way to the jeep, he looked completely like the old Steve, which made Lara's heart lighter.

"Maybe you can," he said, "but not yet. I've got some details to figure out first. Now, let's see that boat."

Lara drove them directly to the dock, got out and walked toward the boat ramp. "That's Jan's," she said, pointing. "The blue one. She leaves the key in it. All of her employees have access on their day off. I'm surprised she hasn't told you about it." Besides Jan's, there were only two other boats docked.

"I haven't had a day off yet," Steve admitted. "Not a full one. Haven't really wanted any. I haven't even thought about it. I've been so thankful for a place to sleep and eat after a month in the remote wilderness of Yellowstone that…"

He trailed off, so she asked, "Why were you in the back country for so long?"

He ignored her question.

The trees were closer to the shore here, except for a section where someone had left a campfire burning and it got away from them. The shore was blackened for a half a mile by the destruction, and Lara turned to tell Steve about the fire, but she found that his attention was on the forest once again.

"This dock is northwest of the lodge, right?" he asked.

"Yes…," Lara answered slowly. Trepidation stirred within her.

"The reservoir flows back into the Snake?"

She nodded. "Henry's Fork, which is part of the Snake."

"Where does it start, again?"

"Less than a mile from here. We can drive to it. It's really quite impressive. Would you like to see?"

He nodded and jumped back into the jeep.

Lara drove, but she couldn't shake a sudden nagging fear. This next stop could confirm her suspicions.

The gravel road to the spillway only took a matter of minutes. Lara stopped at an appropriate point for observation. On one side of the dam the water lapped at enormous boulders lining the road. Steve silently scanned the area, and she watched his gaze follow the water all the way to the dam.

"I can't believe this," he said. Everyone she ever brought here was impressed, but Steve seemed thunderstruck. He even sat in his seat as if afraid to get out and take a closer look. "How deep is the water?"

"At least a hundred feet. They had it drained last fall, and the size of the hole scared me to death. You can get a pretty good idea from this side," Lara pointed out, moving closer. "Come here."

Steve stepped around to where Lara stood looking down; then he stopped dead. Lara heard the air leave his lungs.

"Good God."

"You're right about that," she replied with a laugh. "No one else but God could make such a magnificent place. Certainly not His angels on earth."

They looked down into a vertical canyon. From the dam's mouth, thousands of gallons of tumultuous white water spit into the river, which churned and boiled below.

Steve stared with fascinated horror. "Take me to the spillway," he said.

Lara's anxiety deepened, but she did as he asked.

The reservoir's water flowed smoothly over the edge of a cement construct resembling an immense ditch. When the water reached the cement, it too acquired turbulence, thundering through a giant hole.

"The water drops three hundred feet through that cement cylinder to the canyon below," Lara explained.

"The best waterslide in the world," Steve replied, never removing his eyes. "Has anyone ever rode this sucker and lived?"

Lara felt a shudder run through her. "No one would be stupid enough to try. It would kill them. If a person did live through the ride, he would end up down in Box Canyon."

"And where does the west side of the river lead?"

"The west side…?"

By this time, there was no doubt left in Lara's mind. Steve Mitchell was in danger from something and was planning an escape route. One that would in all probability take his life. She had no idea what he was involved in—she didn't even know what side of the law he was on—but she knew she would help him if she could. He had been everything to her once, and she'd let him down.

She chose her words carefully, so that she wouldn't let on that she knew. Her tone was matter of fact. "The ride would probably kill him, but if he did live, a guy could climb up that steep right bank."

"And what's on that side of the mountain?" Steve asked, staring at the steep slope across from him.

"That section of land is part of Harriman State Park. There are no roads on this end. If you walk far enough, you'll end up on the west end of the reservoir. It's pretty rough terrain. Back in there is where we have the biggest bear population. There's a couple old line shacks, but that's about all."

Steve didn't comment. He just got back into her jeep, saying, "I'd better get back to work."

As they drove past, he peered once more over the edge of Box Canyon. Lara saw him shiver. He was obviously scared to death about whatever plan his mind was hatching, so she was scared to death for him. But she couldn't—wouldn't—lose him again now that she finally had him back in her world.

Chapter Twelve

They drove back to Pond's Lodge, and all afternoon Steve worked on outside projects that Jan gave him. He'd started thinking about his pursuers again, but since he'd done everything he could do he decided to spend the rest of the day thinking of pleasant things. Like Lara. Lara's apology. Her honesty and continued love. Their possible future.

He understood so much more now. Everything, maybe. Although he agreed that some of her thought processes in college had been juvenile and mistaken, he understood—and he forgave. Even better, Lara had never stopped thinking about him in return. She had never stopped loving him. He wanted to hold her until every molecule of pain drifted into outer space or floated away to the ether. He wanted to erase all the hurtful old memories and exchange them for a lifetime of extraordinary experiences neither one of them would ever want to forget. They could really have a life together.

Of course, first he had to get the law off his back. And he had to find their stash.

His pursuers were cops, but they were corrupt California cops, so they shouldn't be able to find him here. Not easily. There were many people living under the radar in these mountains, so his step was light for the moment, his mind and eyes open to the beauty surrounding him. He had a bit of time yet, and so he gazed in wonder at majestic Sawtelle Peak. Maybe he could drive to the top with Lara to see the high alpine wildflowers.

Or, would it be dangerous to be seen anywhere in public with a particular person?

She had invited him to her place for dinner tonight. He felt safe enough to see her there and tell her of his plans. Maybe she could even help. She knew the area and most of its people. Maybe she'd think up something he hadn't. Maybe she'd have a clever plan. With the way he felt right now, he'd have to remind himself to be vigilant.

He spent the end of the afternoon practicing on the small stage in the Pond's Lodge bar. This time he worked up songs he hadn't sung in years, song with romantic lyrics and full of promise.

"I love hearing you sing happy songs for a change," Jan said as Steve strummed his own version of Billy Joel's "She's Got a Way" on his guitar. "You sure seem different this afternoon. Did you and Lara have a good, long…lunch?"

Steve couldn't help but grin. Then, with stronger strums, he answered her question with a rousing rendition of James Brown's "I Feel Good."

Jan danced out of the bar to wait on someone in the store.

* * *

Lara heard the knock at exactly nine p.m. She opened the door, all smiles, and there stood Steve, shrouded in the darkness of the recessed porch.

"Where's your alcove light?" he asked, frowning up into the rafters.

Confused and slightly disappointed, Lara glanced around. This wasn't the warm and welcoming response she'd been hoping for and expecting. She'd felt a heavy load lift since their talk at lunch, and she'd assumed Steve felt a little better about things as well. But this opening comment seemed like nothing had changed.

"It burned out, and I haven't had time to fix it."

Irritation was evident in Steve's voice. "Don't you know how unsafe it is to be without light when you're fumbling for your keys? It wouldn't take two minutes for someone to find out where you live and follow you home."

His sudden rush of concern reminded Lara of her previous concerns. Was he trying to protect her? Would she really need protection from whoever was after him? Who the hell was it, anyway? What had Steve done? What had he gotten himself into, and why was he so afraid?

"I've got an extra bulb in the house," she said. "I'll run get it, and you can help me put it in."

She was back in an instant with a bulb and a chair.

"Don't you have a ladder?" Steve asked.

"No...."

He looked grumpy. "That chair isn't going to work on this uneven rock walkway. I'll have to lift you up."

Lara found no problem with that. She'd take any excuse to be in Steve Mitchell's arms.

She turned her back to him, and his hands slid at once to her waist. Without hesitation he hoisted her to the light. She could feel the muscles in his hands straining under her weight, but she still took her time with the bulb. She was going to make this pleasure last as long as she could.

A grunt from Steve warned her that it might not be a good idea to take *too* long.

"Okay, that's it," she said.

"Thank God. What were you doing up there, rewiring?"

As he eased her slowly back to the ground, Lara put her hands over his and pulled them around the flatness of her belly. His head dipped, and she could feel his soft yet sharply boned masculine cheek on the side of her neck. She waited for a kiss. His warm breath sent vibrations clear to her toes.

His words were as rusty as a spike from an old railroad bed. "You, babe, need to be more careful. You never know what lurks in the night."

Lara was ready to make love right there, standing up. She still faced away from him, but she nestled closer, pressing her bottom into his groin. He wanted her, too. All doubt was erased when she felt the rigid contours of his manhood.

Steve's hands shifted, his palms gliding like feathers over her ribs. Lara arched back, thrusting her bosom forward, willing him to continue his exploration, and his moist lips finally touched the throbbing pulse in her neck. She raised one hand to cup the back of his thick hair then boldly took his hands and moved them to her breasts. Her nipples ached for his touch.

She wanted to show him that she'd grown up. Her need was palpable. She'd waited so long to tell him she was sorry, and now she desperately wanted to tell him with her body. Wanted to show him she was all woman.

"Steve," she whispered while he was still behind her. "Please come in. Please."

She took his hands from around her waist and led him through the front door.

"The bedroom is up those stairs," she said between kisses. He scooped her into his strong arms as if she were a child, placed her on the cushy sofa and swiftly began devouring her. He couldn't get enough.

It was almost as if they had talked about how it would be their first time and both of them already knew their role. She arched her back as he pulled off her pants, and his were off two seconds later. He unbuttoned her blouse just far enough to get to her bra, slid his hand inside and released the creamy white flesh from each cup. The still-clasped bra pushed her tits into fuller, tantalizing orbs, nipples erect.

Devouring her breasts with his lips, Steve slipped his fingers down and gently applied a fluttering motion over her center beneath her already damp panties. Lara could not hold on, and wave after wave of pleasure burst through her. She marveled that something—anything—could feel so good. It was her very first orgasm with a partner, and better than anything she'd ever experienced.

She moaned, and Steve moved his mouth to hers and tugged on her bottom lip. When her climax subsided, Lara gave him an intimate kiss in return, moving her tongue into his mouth and reaching down to touch him. She wanted him inside her now, right now.

Steve's size and hardness surprised her. She couldn't believe she'd waited eighteen years for this! And then he made it happen with one simple, perfect thrust.

Oh good hell, she was going to come again. She could feel it rising rapidly within her as he moved, and the seriousness in Steve's green eyes made her feel alluring and needed and desired, so different than any other experience of her past.

Once again, her spirit soared into climax. Steve joined her within seconds. Although he made little noise, Lara felt the power of his shuddering body, and she knew he too had experienced what she was feeling. They lay together, panting heavily, breathing in unison.

Without turning on a light or dressing, he took her hand and whispered, "Now, pretty lady"—an endearment he'd used when they were dating—"show me to your bed."

Lara couldn't believe it. She was again more comfortable with Steve than she'd ever been with her husband. And so, without embarrassment, she led him up the stairs naked from the waist down.

The two of them in bed, Steve took his time. He slowly unbuttoned her blouse, removed her bra, and just stared for a few minutes with a yearning Lara could feel throughout her body. Her tummy tightened, and she watched him grow hard again.

He removed his t-shirt with one swift motion and crawled over her.

"I don't want to miss a thing," he told her in a rough yet tender growl as he turned on the lamp.

In her entire life, Lara had never felt so sexy, womanly, or wanted. She marveled that she could be naked and lying under this gorgeous man with his thick black hair and beautiful green eyes, this man she'd dreamt about since that terrible fifteen-year-old mistake. He'd given her one moment of wondrous perfection already, and he was ready to have her again.

It was with new courage she went forward into their lovemaking. And when Steve showed her just how much he knew, it was apparent to Lara that at least one of them hadn't been celibate for the past fifteen years.

Now she was reaping the benefits.

* * *

Steve awakened to an all-consuming desire. He was hard, and he wanted one woman and one woman alone. Lara. He'd dreamt of having her all night and now awakened to want her again. Of course, he'd dreamt about having Lara Douglass for years. It's just that this past night's dreams had seemed so real.

Turning over, he realized that he wasn't in his own bed. A dark-haired woman lay next to him, an arm thrown over her eyes.

Dear God, it hadn't been a dream.

As his head began to clear, he suddenly remembered everything. The entire night. It had most certainly not been a dream.

He slowly and gently slid his hand up and under the covers until he felt the warm, soft skin of her shoulder. His touch moved along her cheek, down her neck and over a gorgeous mound of breast, stopping at her nipple and watching in fascination as he teased it to life with his fingers. He caressed her flat belly and marveled at the smoothness, desperately wanting to touch her with his tongue but not wanting to wake her. He must simply study the beauty of her body and get his fill.

After a few minutes he couldn't help but slide his chest closer to her back. He slid his arm underneath her, and while cradling her like that he kissed the back of her tangled hair. Moving his lips to her neck, he felt her stir ever so slightly, so with his free hand he trailed a finger from her breast down her side to her waist, massaging her hip and then her smooth thigh. Soon he was sure she was awake, because her breathing changed—but she didn't say a word, and she didn't move or open her eyes.

He needed her again, and this slow dance was going to speed up. While nibbling on her neck, he placed both hands on her luscious breasts and teased the nipples until they were as erect as he himself. Her eyes fluttered open, and she surprised him by twisting and pushing herself atop him. Rising up, she straddled his manhood, took him in her hand and eased her body down around him. Then, with a brazenness he didn't know she had, she rode him in the early morning light.

Her long hair was tangled, and the closer she got to fulfillment, the wilder she looked. Steve wanted to wait for her, but with her full breasts bouncing above him and her hot, tight, wet body covering him, he was having one hell of a time holding on. He tried to speak, to say something to slow her down, but he couldn't; she was totally in charge and he loved it.

Suddenly, she whispered, *"Now!"*

He released his load, and they came together long and hard.

* * *

Steve Mitchell.

He had turned out to be the lover Lara always imagined: tender, kind, patient, and yet forceful when it was his turn to take charge. Passionate. Experienced. Forgiving. She marveled at his toned body, the thickness of his cock, his strength and endurance. Lara knew now more than ever that he was the man for her. The only man, and she wanted him safe.

While he showered, Lara threw away the wilted salad from the dinner they'd never got around to eating the night before. It had been since their picnic that either had eaten, and she was starved, so she quickly went to work scrambling eggs with mushrooms and cheese thrown in, cooked toast while coffee brewed, and had it all sitting on the table when Steve finally walked down the loft stairs.

Her unanswered questions were driving Lara crazy. She suspected that things were heating up again with whatever Steve was involved in, and she wanted to get him to share his concerns with her. After all, there wasn't anything she could do to help if she had no idea what was happening.

"Sit," she commanded. "Breakfast is ready."

Steve brushed against her as he took his seat. He picked up his coffee cup, but his eyes never left the front of her robe.

Lara pulled it closed and decided to dive right in. "You're very pensive. Didn't you enjoy yourself?"

His eyes caressed every part of her body, but his expression was melancholy. "I smiled a lot last night and this morning, don't you remember? And to answer your unasked question, I am still very much in love with you. Always have been. Always will be."

He shook his head then looked down at his plate for several seconds. Lara held her breath. She instinctively knew things were about to change for them. She waited for the "but"…and sure enough, he finally said it.

"But things are different now. Really different. Last night cemented my feelings for you, and while I showered I thought about it. I now know what I have to do. Under the circumstances, I've got to leave."

Leave? Lara couldn't catch her breath, and she set her coffee mug down with a shaky hand. "What? Why now?"

"I should have left yesterday, or on the Fourth of July, but I just couldn't. Your pull was too strong for me to resist. But I've got to get out of Dodge. For both of our sakes. I have to get back to what I was supposed to be doing all along."

Lara was shocked. She rose from the table and rushed to the seat nearest him. "Please, Steve! Tell me what's going on and let me help."

"Absolutely not, Lara. Not under these circumstances. It is just too dangerous to be connected to me or really know anything."

"That's just it, Steve. Damn it, I don't know anything!"

He sighed. "I'm trying to find a connection in this area to an extremely evil couple of bastards that wouldn't miss one hour of sleep if they killed us both. That's how I got clear into Yellowstone in the first place."

Lara grabbed his forearm and squeezed. She wondered if her face conveyed relief at the this not being about her, or if it showed the shock she felt deep in the pit of her stomach, the small voice in her heart that was screaming about the fact he could be killed.

Instead of freaking out, like she wanted to do, she rose to her feet and went to stand at the sink. Looking out over the calming river, she took a couple of deep breaths and then turned back to face him.

"Okay, Steve, let's take this down to smaller bites. You've got to go over the whole story before I can help. Between Jan and my Uncle Lawrence, they know just about everyone who lives here. They know something about their past, and also a lot about our summer residences. My uncle used to be a NYC cop, and he went on to become a damn good detective. I trust him more than anyone in the world, and Jan also. We've got to get together with them, so you only have to tell your story once."

Steve didn't say anything; he just stared at her.

"I'm not surprised about your problems," she continued. "Jeb said two guys were asking about you. He works down the road thirty miles, so they are close if they haven't already found you. You take a roundabout way back to Pond's and get your things ready to leave the moment you have to. In the meantime, I'll get Jan and my uncle to meet us back here in an hour. We'll make a plan from there."

Steve began to protest, but Lara ran nude up the loft stairs, leaving her fluffy bathrobe on the kitchen floor.

Chapter Thirteen

An hour later, Steve and Lara, her Uncle Lawrence and Jan sat around Lara's kitchen table. Jan looked confused, but Lawrence's expression was that of a concerned parent waiting for bad news.

"We haven't got much time here," Lara stated, "but we need to help Steve. He's going to explain what he can, and then he's got to leave. I think."

Steve sighed. "I don't have a lot of time for all the details, but here's the basic history. I'm with the FBI. I've been chasing two crooked cops for months. I followed my marks to West Yellowstone. We have evidence that they got wind of a huge drug ring that was going to make a big sale and, instead of reporting it, they decided to watch for the buy and take the money for themselves. They've already killed a close friend of mine who was also an agent, and if they've killed one FBI agent, they won't give a rat's ass about killing another. They know that, if they're caught, they're going away for life.

"We are sure that they have inside help, because their own department wasn't able to catch them. I decided to follow the money, which is what led me to West Yellowstone. I was showing their pictures and asking around West when I saw them looking my truck over. McKay actually got in! I chose to head off into the forest because I knew they had discovered I was following them. A couple of nights I tried to get back to my truck, but they were always there. So, I stayed on the mountain for awhile and then came back a different route. That's when Lara found me hitchhiking. I called our headquarters and they said some of the money was reportedly in The Bank of Idaho in Island Park. My assignment was to stay here and try to find out if they were somewhere in the area, and what connection they could possibly have here. After all, there's a whole hell of a lot of mountains to hide your money in closer to L.A. than here.

"Yesterday a construction worker came into the bar and said that two men were looking for a guy with long hair and a full beard, and that his name was Steve. So, needless to say, they've found out who and where I am. I think they're coming to kill me before I can find the money."

"What kind of money are we talking about?" Lawrence asked.

"Four million and change."

Jan whistled. Lara got up to pour coffee, her hands shaking violently.

Lawrence seemed unfazed. "Have you got their names?"

"McKay and Johnson."

"There's a family of McKays that comes here every summer. Well, I think old man McKay died a few years ago in Pocatello, but the rest of the relatives still come. Let me do some snooping around." Lawrence leaned toward Steve. "I don't want to tell you how to play this, as I was a detective many years ago, but here's my suggestion. It's been my experience that with this kind of money at stake, they aren't going to leave much in any one spot, at least not a bank. I'll go over and ask the bank manager what the policy of the Bank of Idaho is, but I think they have to report any deposit of more than twenty thousand or more to the main office. My guess is that, if this McKay guy is involved, that money will be in a hole somewhere."

"That's exactly what I'm afraid of," Steve said. "After living in the backwoods for three weeks, I can honestly say that I could hide money here and never find it again. And the money has to be in this area somewhere, or why would they come and stay around so long? Well, apart from finding and killing me." He laughed. "So, Lawrence, what would you suggest I do while you're asking questions at the bank—if I'm not going to make a break for it and watch them from another location?"

"Do you have an escape plan ready if they find you? You need a way to really give them the slip."

Steve looked up at Lara. He must have seen the fear in her face because he said, "Lara, I've been in bad situations before." He turned back to Lawrence. "It won't be easy, but I do have a plan. That's why I thought it was okay to stay in one place. Well, *one* reason." He glanced at Lara. "Unfortunately, if they're sure they've found me, it will likely be only hours before they pounce."

"Well, let's hope they haven't found you, then—or that your plan works." Lawrence glanced across the table at his niece. His grey eyes filled with unshed tears, and Jan touched his hand. "I really don't want to see Lara terrified about losing the man she's loved since high school."

No one spoke for a few seconds, and then Steve stood. "I've loved her for that long, too, sir, and I've got more to live for now than ever. If something bad happens…well, I will try everything in my power to get back to you, babe," he promised, kissing the top of Lara's head.

Lara was too scared even to cry. She looked at the two men, Lawrence and Steve, the only two men she'd really loved since her father passed away, and she couldn't speak.

Lawrence rose to his feet and shook Steve's hand. "Good luck, son. Let me know what else we can do to help."

The four of them set about planning further. They knew from Jeb that the two guys were looking for a long-haired hippie with a full beard, so Steve's new look helped. That in mind, the four of them decided that, while Lawrence did some investigating, everything else would stay the same. Lara would work as usual at the TroutHunter. Jan was to run Pond's Lodge and keep her eyes and ears open, and Steve would carry on with his normal chores. There were many strangers traveling through Island Park this time of year, so changes might be reported by anyone. They also had to be careful about how and where they talked about what they learned. Other than the four of them, there wasn't anyone they could wholly trust.

When they were done planning, everyone went their separate ways.

The day dragged on for Steve. He hoped that, now with everything ready, the criminals would just get on with it.

He wasn't disappointed. It was late afternoon. Steve was polishing the last of the tables and chairs when he heard Jan's resonant voice even louder than usual, and she almost yelled her next words. "Steve who?"

Her nervousness could be felt from the other room, and Steve knew she was trying to warn him. He quietly set his rag down and raced to the back door. His only hope was to get far enough ahead of the men to lead them into the oncoming evening.

The sun slipped over the Centennial Mountains, and Steve remembered he'd promised to get back to Lara in one piece. He wanted nothing more than to make all of her dreams come true, and he prayed now as he ran that he would have another day to do it.

It's funny what a person thinks about in a crisis. Steve's labored breathing poured pressure onto his heart, his thighs burned and his mouth felt like someone had wiped it out with a towel, but his thoughts as he ran through the lodge pole pines were of the dessert his mother used to make him in high school: lemon pound cake and a tall glass of cold milk. He had no idea why that thought came into his mind; maybe it was simply the fact that his mother had always made it for him when he was having a stressful day…and he was definitely having one of those right now. It was one that he had actually planned for, but he still wasn't sure that everything would work out.

In the twilight he could see the water sparkling beyond the edge of the forest. If he could only find the boat dock from here…

A sudden movement in front of him stopped Steve dead in his tracks. The pain in his chest from running increased when he stood still, and the hammering intensified as her realized he'd forgotten to grab the backpack sitting by the back door. How could he have forgotten that pack? It was a stupid rookie mistake. If he died, he would damn well deserve it.

A startled doe and her fawn leapt across his path, moving deeper into the woods.

His tension subsided—and then returned as, somewhere in the distance, he heard a tree branch crunch behind him. He began to run again, harder than before.

Where was the dock? The landscape looked so different on foot and at dusk. Could he get to the boat? More importantly, would it still be there?

Trying to catch his breath, Steve stopped momentarily and glanced behind him. He had no idea if the men were pursuing him on foot or by car, but he was certain they were coming one way or another.

Night was fast approaching. Steve knew he must hurry or he wouldn't be able to see the boat even if it was there.

Another clatter from behind him spurred Steve into rapid movement.

"Quiet," he heard a rusty voice whisper. "I think I heard him."

They were close—too damn close. In the weeks he had tracked these men, Steve had never gotten equally close. If he stayed right where he stood, they would be on him in a matter of seconds. If he fled they would hear.

He ran.

Surprisingly, the terrain altered, and for a few hundred yards the trees disappeared. Steve's feet touched gravel, and he knew he was in the parking lot of the dock. With renewed energy he sprinted forward.

He found Jan's little aluminum boat tied up right next to another craft. It wouldn't be very fast, but it would be a hell of a lot faster than swimming. He started the sluggish motor and pulled away just as he heard his enemies step onto the ramp behind him. Within seconds they were in another boat that had been tied next to Jan's at the dock.

The night was pitch-black, but he had to think about the next part of his escape. Trepidation filled every cell of his body. He prayed that he would be able to see the spillway before he passed it.

There. He could barely make out the place that would make or break him in the next few seconds, but maybe it was for the best. He remembered Lara's words when he'd asked if anyone had ever jumped into the boiling waters of the deep cement cauldron.

"Are you kidding? It would kill you!"

"Well, my sweet love, I hope you're wrong."

He jumped.

Chapter Fourteen

Lara hadn't yet heard from either Steve or her uncle, and at seven o'clock, as she checked in guests at the TroutHunter, she thought back to the previous evening, to before she and Steve made love when she'd caught an expression of desolation on his face.

There were a few times she'd felt as if he were still trying to separate himself from her, despite all that was happening between them, but each time she recognized the signs he pulled back out of his moodiness. She'd decided to let the issue go.

By nine o'clock she let the night manager take over and drove herself home. A glass of wine usually calmed her nerves, but tonight it didn't and she decided she couldn't wait any longer. She walked with slow, measured steps to Steve's tiny home.

No lights. Her stomach churned.

She tried the door. It wasn't locked.

Maybe he'd decided to leave and take his trouble as far from her as he could get. That'd be just like him, taking the whole decision on himself. Swallowing hard, Lara opened the door and prayed that wasn't the case. She didn't think she could bear it.

She turned on the light. The bed covers lay in a crumpled heap as if he had just left them, and Steve's clothes were hung over the tiny cabin's lone chair. A sigh escaped her pursed lips, but Lara's relief lasted only an instant before the heavy, weathered door was flung wide and she spun to see Jan in the entrance.

"Lara. There you are."

The look on her friend's face made Lara grow icy with fear. "What's happened? Where's Steve?"

Jan shook her head. "I don't know. Two men came into the store and demanded to know where he was. They knew he works for me. When I acted as if I didn't know him, one of them grabbed my arm so tight that…" She lifted the sleeve of her T-shirt to show where an ugly bruise darkened her skin. "I yelled, 'Steve who?' Then the back door slammed and they were out of there like a shot. Steve couldn't have had more than a two-minute head start."

Lara wanted to scream or cry, anything to relieve the torment rampaging through her heart. It wasn't fair. She had finally regained the love of her life, and now two strangers were intent on snatching him away.

Through the fog in her mind, she heard Jan talking again.

"Which way did they go?" she interrupted. "I mean, when they left." She was amazed that she could think at all, but she had no time to feel sorry for herself. Someone else's life was in jeopardy, and that someone just happened to be most important person in the whole world to her. "Did the two men give their names?"

"They didn't say, and there was no time to ask." Jan paused, and the look on her face swamped Lara with another sick wave of dread. "But, there's something else. They asked me if Steve has a girlfriend. It seems like there are rumors circulating that he does. I said I couldn't help them but…"

Lara let the cold fear pass right through her, and then she shrugged. "It's all right, Jan. They must not know for sure it's me, at least not yet. And Steve got a head start, even if it was a small one. Did he get his backpack?"

"Oh my God. I didn't even think to look."

They hurried to the back entrance of Pond's. There, on the ground, lay Steve's pack. The supplies he'd need to last a few days in the wilds were in that pack, as well as his gun.

"Jan," Lara said quickly. "I know this looks bad, but I also know Steve. He had a plan, and even without his pack he can make this work. I do not intend on losing him now. We'll get through this somehow, and then, when this is all over, we will begin a new life together. Steve and I. Finally."

She searched Jan's eyes for the reassurance she needed, and her friend's weak smile turned into a broad grin.

"Come here," Jan said, and she threw her arms around Lara in a comforting hug. "I love him, too, honey. How could anyone not? I think it's the universe saying something, you two finding each other again after all these years, and I just love happy endings. So let's get our butts in gear and make a plan of action. We'll see this through together."

Lara spent the rest of the night gathering supplies for Steve to hide out in the wilderness. She refused to consider that he might have been killed or caught. She didn't know what his next step would be, so she had to be ready for anything. But she had to find him before she could help him.

The next morning, a man from Bill's Island found Jan's boat wrecked against his dock. No one was in it. It was a good thing that she'd had an idea of what Steve intended, as the debris confirmed Lara's assumption: He had tried to jump into the spillway. If he'd survived, he'd be headed to the line shack—which meant she had to get to him as soon as possible. There would be no provisions there to sustain him. She needed to disappear, herself. It was only a matter of time before Steve's pursuers' questions put her and Steve together, so this trip would kill two birds with one stone.

She had learned from her uncle that McKay and Johnson actually registered at the TroutHunter after she left for the night. They had checked in around one o'clock in the morning looking wet, exhausted, and muddy. He also told her that McKay was indeed part of the family that lived in the nearby neighborhood of Shotgun. He had been coming to Island Park every year since he was a child. For three summers he'd even worked at the Shotgun store.

With the fact that they'd check into The TroutHunter, Lara surmised that the pair must know something about her connection to Steve. She assembled all the supplies that she felt were essential: a first-aid kit, binoculars, sleeping bags, a small pack stove, food, etc. Most of what she needed she found already bundled in Steve's room. Another backpack was partially filled, as if he'd known the time would come when he would have to flee. It was no wonder he'd always seemed to be just a little on edge.

Lara stuffed everything she could into a duffel bag and tied the two sleeping bags onto an aluminum frame; she would travel as light as possible on the hike to the line shack. Her first instinct had been to start her trek immediately, but Jan wisely reasoned Lara knew this country better than the men who might follow her, and she would be much harder to follow in the darkness. But, waiting was almost impossible. Lara's soul now required Steve's presence. She couldn't experience joy without him. Her only goal was to find him, make him comfortable, and be by his side once again. To be there for him in every way he ever needed. In every way he might ever want.

She pushed the fear away from her mind again as she contemplated the fact that Steve might not be in the tiny line shack. He had to be. There was no other place on that mountain he could hide.

Steve's pursuers were now based at the TroutHunter, and she didn't dare go to her house, so Lara ended up hiding in Jan's cabin a mile from the Lodge. Lara paced Jan's living room in agitated silence. Would the sun never set? Was Steve okay? How long would it take for her to find him?

She folded her arms and tried to keep a chill of apprehension from the rest of her body. It had been almost twenty-four hours since Steve left. Her uncle, listening to their conversation, had extrapolated that his pursuers were waiting for a body to be discovered either in the reservoir or at the head of Box Canyon. If that happened, they believed, their danger would be over. From what Lawrence gathered, they just needed to kill Steve.

They had heard he'd made friends with a woman who lived in the area, and they thought she worked at the TroutHunter. Their best bet would be to find and follow her, they said. However, they didn't know her name or where she lived.

Lara began to mentally prepare for her hike to the line shack. Because it didn't lead to much of anything, the trail was used very seldom. She herself had hiked it only once, with her uncle and father who'd heard that a brown bear and her cubs were on the hillside, and who wanted to take pictures and try to sell them to an outdoor magazine. They'd walked right to the top of three mountains but never saw any bear. Lara hoped she would be as fortunate tonight.

Dusk approached late in the evening at this time of year, and it was almost nine before Jan and Lara slipped through the growing darkness and loaded gear into Jan's truck. Jan had helped Lara dress in men's clothing, right down to covering her riotous hair with a bandanna and baseball cap. Given the rumors, Steve's pursuers would be likely looking for a female—someone with long hair.

Neither Lara nor Jan said much as they traveled the two miles to the trailhead, and Lara's hope plummeted as they traveled past the spillway. Could Steve have really survived, or was his body torn and broken on the jagged rocks of the river?

Jan read her mind. "Don't even think it. He's on the mountain. I promise you. A fisherman would have found him by now if he were still in the water."

Lara gazed out the window and prayed she was right.

They hid Jan's vehicle behind a clump of ancient blue spruces, and Jan helped Lara slip on the cumbersome backpack.

"Now, give me a hug for luck."

There was nothing else to say. They had gone over the plan a hundred times, but what it all boiled down to was the fact that Lara had to find Steve. If he wasn't in the shack, there was no further plan.

"Thanks for everything, Jan." Lara could have gone on and on, but she knew her friend would be uncomfortable hearing any sugary gratitude, so she turned and trudged away up the insanely steep path leading through the thick forest. She heard Jan get in her truck and head back to Pine's Lodge.

The half-moon was up, giving off an eerie blue-grey glow. Lara looked back down the path. She could see no signs of life, but she had only gone a few hundred yards. She hoped no one had caught sight of her leaving, but she couldn't be sure; surely the men would be smart enough to stay out of sight for a while. So, a flashlight was out of the question. Any fool could follow a beam.

The trail was tangled with wild weeds and thick clumps of grass. After a mile or so, Lara decided that no one had used this path for years and there was absolutely no sense in wasting time trying to pick her way along it; she could reach the summit much faster if she hiked straight up.

It wasn't long after she shifted her heavy load and headed up the mountain in a new direction that she briefly wondered if she'd made the right choice. The level of difficulty had increased tremendously. She stumbled every few feet over dirt piles and fallen timber. Stiff pine branches scraped her cheeks and tangled with her pack, but she pushed on, intent to get to the man she loved.

To keep her mind from the grueling climb, Lara fantasized of the reception she would receive. First, a look of incredulous joy as Steve swept her into his arms and kissed her passionately. Then, in a thousand different ways, he would tell her of his undying love.

A movement to her side stopped all fantasy. She wasn't really afraid of being hurt by Steve's pursuers, at least not yet, not if they were following her to find Steve, but—

Before she could balance herself on the steep incline, an enormous bull elk leapt in front of her. Lara teetered precariously, her nose close enough to smell the beast. The bull's impressive head bent down, as if he planned on charging, so Lara had no choice but to take a step back. Her high-top boot slid on a dewy log, and she fell end over end back down the way she had come.

A Douglas fir, thirty inches in diameter, finally broke Lara's fall. She sat dazed for several minutes, not daring to move for fear of finding something broken. Her tailbone felt crushed and a burning pain shot up her spine, that fire spreading throughout her body. She had lost her pack somewhere along the way, and her left arm felt as if a boxer had used her for punching practice.

Gingerly she moved her extremities, starting with her toes and working her way up. She didn't think anything was broken. She prayed she was right.

Something warm oozed from her arm, from several of her fingers and the side of her face. She guessed it was blood, but she couldn't see very clearly in the dim light of the moon. And, scrapes and cuts could wait. She had to locate her pack.

It took her twenty minutes to find the supplies. Luckily, they were in better shape than Lara. Placing the pack on her damaged back made her want to cry out in pain, but she saved her energy for the walk. The thing that disgusted her most was how she'd lost time and a hundred feet or more in the climb. And if the men were anywhere on the mountain, they would surely have heard her fall.

* * *

A short time later, a heavy cloud had covered the moon, making the night pitch-black.

"Son of a bitch," Lara said out loud, and then she forcibly wondered at her choice of cursing. Whoever coined that phrase, and what had been the first son of a bitch? A puppy?

Ten more steps, she told herself. Salty tears stung the cuts on her cheeks as they trickled silently to her chin. Her rear throbbed. She was absolutely sure her tailbone was shattered. She ached violently, she was exhausted, and worst of all she was hopelessly lost. If she didn't see or hear something familiar soon she was just going to sit down on her broken butt and give up.

Twenty steps later, Lara did just that.

Feeling around in the depths of the backpack, she found a candy bar and opened the wrapper. She couldn't read the label, but a bite of the Hershey's Cookies and Mint was her first and only pleasure in the last four hours.

Lara felt a strange surge of hope fill her veins, and she tried to analyze why. Chocolate had always given her the warm fuzzies, but to make her feel good at this dreadful moment was amazing. If she ever got off this godforsaken mountain she'd have to give Mr. and Mrs. Hershey a call and thank them. And then, suddenly, better than any chocolate on earth, Lara realized why she'd had the surge of energy. She was sitting on flat ground. There hadn't been a foot of level earth since she'd left Jan's truck. She must have accidentally stumbled her way to the top of the peak!

Finding the shack in darkness was impossible, so Lara laid her head on her pack and willed the clouds to move from blocking the natural light of the moon. She guessed it was almost an hour before they decided to give her a little help.

Painfully, Lara rose to her feet and looked around. She'd been right. She stood on the crest of the mountain. To the west she could make out the dark outline of Island Park Reservoir, so from this point she couldn't be more than a quarter of a mile to the shack.

She'd have to hurry. Dawn was fast approaching, and she wanted to be out of sight before daylight.

Luckily, the terrain was easier on top. Ranchers had cleared sections of the mountain for better grazing for their animals, and spurred on, Lara quickened her pace. At another time she would have reveled in the first rays of daybreak, but today they were merely a reminder of how long it had taken her to reach her destination. Still, she felt a burst of happiness upon seeing the tin roof gleaming in the faint morning light.

Eyes straight ahead, using the shelter as her guide, Lara shifted into a brisk walk. Every joint throbbed and her rear end offered a constant burning ache, but her concern for Steve was far greater than her own discomfort. And then, as if she were living in a slow-motion nightmare, the inconceivable happened.

Lara felt her feet sink into the earth, like quicksand only crunchy. She heard the sickening sound of something snapping, and her body suddenly lay at a crazy angle in comparison to her leg.

This can't be happening.

Nauseated, she bit her lower lip to keep from screaming in pain. If Steve was in the cabin he would definitely hear her, but so would anyone else.

After several minutes, Lara's head cleared enough for her to pull herself into a sitting position and she was somewhat relieved to see that her leg was not broken. Upon further examination, there were snapped twigs lying all around, and the pain centered in her ankle. And as she eased her foot from a hole, she realized for the first time that she had fallen into a trap—a man-made trap. She vowed to someday find the creep who had set this trap and do permanent damage to his person. Trapping was illegal here!

She carefully removed her hiking boot. Instantly, her ankle swelled to three times its original size.

"Damn it to hell and back!" She should have never taken off the boot.

Grabbing hold of a prickly pine branch above her head, she tried to stand. The pain was so intense that she swooned. Putting weight on that pulsating ankle was out of the question, so Lara sat back down, ripped the sleeve off of her flannel shirt and tightly wrapped her injury.

Angrily finding a long stick on the ground, she slowly rose to her feet and used it as a crutch. Then she limped steadily toward the shack, a swearword on her lips every step of the way.

The shelter looked deserted, and Lara's heart felt heavy in her chest. All of this for nothing. She wondered how many days she would have to wait until Jan and her uncle came looking for her. With her leg in this shape, she was never going to walk off this mountain.

And if Steve wasn't here, did that mean he was dead?

She hobbled to the door. It was hanging at a lopsided angle, the bottom hinge missing. Lara pressed her palm against the wood and instantly recognized the rough texture of bear claw marks, and it took all her strength to lift it enough to enter the cabin's musty and shadowy interior.

A shudder of apprehension surged through her weakened body, but she hobbled only one step more before she felt a sharp blow to the head. Then she didn't feel anything.

Chapter Fifteen

God, was Lara going to be mad when she woke up.

Steve still couldn't believe she was lying there. He could have cried when he turned the body over and discovered her. How had she known where he would be? The last thing he'd wanted was for her to get involved. Nevertheless, he had never loved anyone more for trying.

She had changed so much since high school. She'd been so timid then, so unsure of herself. Now here she was, hiking straight uphill with a thirty-pound pack on her back, all in the name of trying to help him. Speaking of that, he strode restlessly to the window and once again scanned the horizon. He hoped and prayed for both of their sakes that she hadn't been followed.

Kneeling beside her, Steve painstakingly removed the wrap from Lara's ankle. The bruised area had turned hideous shades of blue and black. With no ice to help, he had to rely on the pressure of the rags to fight the swelling. He tended to her many scrapes, as well as the knot on her head he'd given her. With gentle fingers he touched that bump again. It had decreased considerably, and he was thankful that the blow hadn't broken the skin.

As his hand probed deeper into the tangled mass of Lara's dark hair, checking to see exactly how much damage he had caused, Lara's soft moan startled him. Her eyes fluttered open, she looked at him with a half smile, as if she were dreaming, and then they shut again.

Steve straightened one sleeping bag underneath her, pulled the other atop her, and then sat cross-legged on the dirty, wooden floor and watched her face. His rough fingertip brushed her scratched cheek. He hoped there wouldn't be a scar, and yet, if there was, it would be a constant reminder of how much she'd risked for him. He hadn't known this kind of unconditional love from anyone but his parents.

Remembering his parents made him sick to his stomach. He'd hated not telling them the danger of the case he was working on, but he didn't want to put their lives in danger. He hadn't been able to call them now for almost two months. How surprised they'd be when they heard from him again! He hoped that, if he and Lara got out of this alive, his parents would welcome her back with open arms. His mother had been angry at the time they broke up, but at least she hadn't said bad things about her, at least not to him. His mother had always known how much he loved Lara.

Love. Not only his past, but his chosen line of work had left him disillusioned with the human race, especially when it came to matters of the heart. He firmly believed the organ was generally fickle. He had witnessed almost every kind of cruelty and deceit— much in the name of love. And yet, his parents' loving marriage always brought him back to center; to hope. And now the simplicity of his life in Island Park and Lara's recently demonstrated devotion threatened to drastically change his attitude. For the first time in years, he actually wanted to believe in hope and joy. If only he could end this miserable case, he and Lara could make a new start.

She shifted to the right, turning toward him, her movements sluggish and tormented, and she moaned. This time, she opened first one eye and then the other.

"Oh."

Steve waited for her head to clear. He thought he could detect adoration in those eyes, but...now it was recognition.

"You dirty son of a bitch!"

* * *

Before the dark curtain fell, Lara had benefited from a second to see what was happening—and who was doing it to her. Her subsequent dreams were sweet, but she hadn't forgotten a thing. Not a damn thing.

"Just what in the hell were you thinking?" she demanded of Steve. The pain in her ankle ceased to exist now that her throbbing head had taken over.

"I'm so sorry, babe."

He lifted his hand to her forehead, but she found enough strength to push it away. "Don't call me that. Babe is Paul Bunyan's blue ox. My name is Lara. I'm on your side, remember?"

Steve looked irked. "How was I supposed to know you'd be coming dressed as a man? How was I supposed to know you'd be coming at all?"

His voice rose dramatically, and then his jaw clamped shut as if he suddenly remembered he wanted to keep quiet. Lara knew he was trying to control his temper. He was probably also beginning to realize what she must have been through to find him.

"How's your ankle?" he asked, softer. "I can't tell from looking if it's sprained or broken."

Lara raised herself up on her elbows and looked toward her feet. Steve had wrapped her ankle with his flannel shirt. She tried to sit up, but spasms in her tailbone demanded that she lay back down.

"I stepped into a stupid trap."

Steve paled.

Lara rolled onto her side and glared at him in astonishment. "*You* did that! You made that damn trap, didn't you?" She knew the answer, but she wanted to hear it from his mouth.

"It was for my protection. I had to make do with what the land has to offer. I don't have a weapon. I stupidly left everything back at the bar." He looked sheepish once more. "Thanks for bringing my backpack and all that other stuff. I can't believe I left it. I think my brain has been addled with thoughts of you."

"Thank God you didn't have your gun or I could have been dead!" Lara grumbled, rubbing the tender spot on her head. "At the very least I'd be nursing a bullet wound right now."

"I never shoot to wound," he said seriously.

Lara didn't think that made her feel any better.

Steve rose again and strode to the window, clearly looking for unwanted guests. Glancing down at her foot, Lara began to tremble. Then she filled him in on everything Lawrence had found out, and the fact that he'd bugged McKay and Johnson's rooms.

Steve's back grew rigid, but he didn't turn to face her. "Do they know you're involved with me?"

"They know you're seeing a woman, but as far as my uncle knows they don't have my name or what I look like."

"God, Lara. This is the last thing I wanted. I should have stayed away from you. I…"

He paused, clearly berating himself. And yet, she knew why he couldn't stay away. She felt the same. And she wanted to hear the words.

He came back to where she lay on her cushion of sleeping bags, reached up and touched her freed hair. "Lara, you're my center of gravity. I'm continuously pulled into your stream of energy."

Lara's breath quickened with the intensity she saw in his eyes. The sun, peeking through the tiny window, warmed her aching back as Steve reached out and touched her cheek.

"Even when you weren't with me, I was drawn to your memory. Do you know, my love, that I thought of you at least once every single day since I left you sitting up in that bed fifteen years ago? For a long time all I could remember was that image. The way your dark hair spilled down across your breasts, the tears running down your cheeks…. The sad but honest way you nodded when I asked if you'd wanted him to…" He closed his eyes. "I couldn't get it out of my head. God, I felt like such a fool. To love someone like I loved you, only to find that you wanted another man…."

His finger moved down Lara's cheek and neck, sliding across the top of her breast to finally reach her jutting nipple. She shuddered at that delicate touch, remembering their recent night and morning together, how he had licked and sucked and caressed her. How they had finally achieved all they had waited so many years to experience—or perhaps just the start of things to come.

She felt a pressure building in the center of her, and she wanted him again. She moved closer and pushed her breasts into Steve's fingers, but as she arched her back, a pain shot through her so sharp that it took her breath away.

He continued talking, unaware. "How I'd dreamed of seeing you naked like that, but in my fantasies it was always me you'd chosen." He pulled back, as if his hand were scorched by his memory. "I drove that night, drove for hundreds of miles, and when I knew that I was far enough away that I wouldn't be able to kill Philip I pulled off the road and cried like a baby."

Steve. Stillness surrounded them in the shack, and through her tears Lara watched dust particles dance in rays of morning sunshine. She longed to erase the pain she had caused that boy so long ago.

But a man was here in that boy's place, and she vowed to repent and make him whole again. She vowed to be everything he would ever need for as long as he would have her.

"I am so glad you forgave what I did as a girl," she whispered. "And that I get to know you as a man."

Resting her hand on his crotch, she felt him stir to life once more. He eyed her, and his mouth quirked up in a grin.

"Speaking of growing, I love your grown-up breasts. Did Phillip pay for those?"

She swatted at him. "I swear to God, if I could get up I'd beat the shit out of you right now. These are one hundred percent natural and you know it!" She quickly unbuttoned her shirt and lifted her sports bra. "Don't you remember? Touch them. There's nothing fake about me. These are God-given, and they're all mine. And yours if you want them."

Steve's grin faded so that only desire clouded his green eyes. Lara read that lust and wiggled ever so slightly, tantalizing him further. Then, before she could count to two, he had one nipple in his mouth and the other between his rough fingertips, and he ravished them until she felt herself pulsing with desire.

Her injuries were forgotten; she needed to release this pent-up energy. She was in pain all right, but it wasn't from her tailbone or ankle. Her breath coming in excited pants, she slipped her hand down to the bulge in his jeans and felt Steve throb beneath the zipper. She moved to release and stroke his raging heat.

He slid two fingers to the seam of her jeans. Pushing harder against his fingers, she pulled on the nipple Steve released to rub her womanhood. Her climax was hard and fierce, and she moaned loudly, never taking her hand from his erection.

Seconds after she came, Steve groaned and did the same. She held him in her hand until he was spent.

Chapter Sixteen

A myriad of birds chirped and sang outside in the ancient firs. Their peaceful song gave Lara hope.

"Steve…," she said. She had hurt him in the past, and she understood how much. But now she could prove her loyalty. She'd already made a good start. After all of this was over, they would make a beautiful life together. "Tell me about your life after you left school."

He glanced over at her. "I roamed around for a while, picking up odd jobs. I guess I was trying to decide what to do next. I had a goddamn time separating me from us. Everything revolved around you and our dreams." He paused. "As you know, music was my first love, so I went to Nashville…but I could see there that I was just a very small flash in a large pan unless I learned to write my own songs. And, well, the music was gone. At least, I couldn't come up with anything original."

Lara stared at him, but he shrugged as if it didn't matter.

"I moved back near my parents and enrolled at UCLA. After I got my bachelor's, I decided I wanted to help people, to right wrongs. I figured the best way to do that was to go to the police academy. There I worked my way up to detective, and my partner and I solved a couple of big drug cases. After that I was contacted by the FBI. So I went to Quantico." Suddenly looking uncomfortable, he interrupted himself. "Here, take a few sips of water. Are you hungry?"

Lara shook her head. "Go on."

Steve sighed. "Business was great. I traveled the nation nabbing bad guys and 'righting wrongs.' But I stopped beginning relationships. I couldn't see the point. It seemed like every living person over the age of ten was a waste. I've seen too much crap—

adultery, abuse, incest, murder, drugs, you name it. I've got a hundred stories about each. So *many* wrongs. Somewhere along the line I despaired."

Every emotion seemed to play across Steve's face. He had lived his life on the dark side, and the sun rarely warmed his soul. Lara's heart ached for him and all those years he'd spent away from her, but she didn't say anything; she just reached out and slowly stroked his arm.

He glanced at her. "This time in Island Park with you has made me rethink that."

Lara was glad. She didn't want to interrupt him, though, so she just smiled.

Steve sighed again then combed his fingers through his thick, dark hair. "I've put most of my money in the bank. I didn't have time to spend it on much of anyone or anything. I've accumulated quite a large sum over the years." He tickled her side and his deep green eyes looked into hers, and she saw a twinkle of humor there. "Did you hear me? I'm rich. Does that make me a little more appealing?"

The money meant little to Lara at this point in her life, if it might have turned her head when she was younger. If she could have Steve for the rest of her days, that would be enough. Still, she played along with his teasing. She adored him when he smiled like that.

"Are you kidding?" she said. "You're looking better to me every minute."

Steve laughed, but his grin faded quickly. "I guess the only problem is living long enough to get it out of the bank."

The sober timbre of his voice brought Lara back to reality. She knew there was a lot more to his story, and she wanted to hear. "Tell me about your partner that was killed."

Steve sat up and wrapped the string on the sleeping bag cover around his finger several times. "They assigned me to Special Agent Jim Higgins and a group from the FBI who were working a big case. I won't go into the nitty-gritty, because it'd be surprisingly boring, but we started at the bottom with one drug dealer and worked our way up to find corruption in a police department. It was just a matter of finding who was dirty and who was clean."

He took a deep breath. "We began working overtime and finally followed the evidence to two detectives named McKay and Johnson.

One night, I left Jim at ten o'clock. An hour later I got a call that he died in a car crash on his way home." Steve's eyes held unshed tears, and he gulped a couple of times before continuing. "He had three great kids and a cute wife. They had one of the few marriages that worked. That crash was no accident. Jim's brakes were tampered with. The only thing I couldn't figure out was why they didn't kill me too. I knew just as much."

He shook his head, clearly remembering. "We had discovered lots of evidence against McKay and Johnson, but we also knew they had friends in high places, including a few in the Bureau. It wouldn't be an easy prosecution. We needed to find the money from that recent deal, which our prosecutor said would be the final nail in their coffin—that we couldn't fail to put them away if we found it. I believe Jim found the key the night he died. The only clue I saw among his things, though—in his trashcan—was a yellow sticky with the words 'West Yellowstone Airport.' So, since I vowed on Jim's grave that I would see those detectives dead or behind bars, I came right up here."

The details of the case had rolled through Lara's ears almost unheard. All she could think of was how much Steve suffered. She rubbed her hand over his back and said simply, "I'm so sorry. About your friend, about all that's happened to you."

Steve nodded. Clearly uncomfortable, he checked her ankle then laid it back down. It felt a little better, the throbbing had lessened somewhat, but it was still extremely painful.

Lara glanced up and saw his face was a stern mask. It led her to say, "It must be extremely depressing for you, trying to make the world a better place. But at least you're making a difference."

Steve glared at her. "Oh hell, Lara. My job is like stepping on a single ant when there's a thousand hills clear full of them."

She saw his point. "And now the ants are trying to step on you."

"Us," he corrected. "God, Lara, I wish I'd never let you get involved. They want me dead, and they'll do anything to see me that way before I find that money—including harm the people I care about. The things we learned they did to cover their trail..." Steve started fumbling in her bag for food. "Will you eat something, please?"

Lara knew he was just trying to help. "I'll have some water and a piece of beef jerky, please."

Steve handed her a stick of dried meat and chewed on one himself as he continued.

"I flew to West Yellowstone, not sure how to follow Jim's clue. After asking a bunch of questions, I decided to go into the park. I bought supplies, food, camping gear, all the stuff I'd need for an extended stay. I didn't know where I was going, but I prayed I'd get lucky. I stopped at Old Faithful to ask some more questions and watch the geyser...and damn near ran right into McKay. He walked right past me."

Lara gasped. "Someone must have been watching over you, Steve. What a lucky break. That parking lot is *huge*. A person could lose their car in it."

Steve shook his head, as if he couldn't believe his fortune at seeing the detective, either—especially before he was himself seen. "I was lucky, yeah, so I got in my truck and waited with binoculars. I watched McKay. He went up to Johnson and handed him an ice cream cone, and then they watched the geyser shoot hot water ninety feet into the air, all as if they weren't a couple of goddamn murderers and thieves. Then they got into a rental car."

Lara sat forward, wondering what happened next.

"I followed them back to West Yellowstone. That's when I saw them scoping out my truck, as I was coming back from the public restrooms. Somehow I'd given myself away. They were on to me, and I knew what they'd do if they got me alone. I couldn't leave the area, though, not if I wanted to find their stash, and they didn't leave my car for two days, so I hitched my backpack to my shoulder—I'd taken it with me when I left the truck—and started walking south into the mountains."

Lara just stared at him. "And then—?"

"I didn't stop to rest for another two days. Both men are in good shape, so I figured they might catch me if they saw me leave, but I hoped they hadn't and would wait a longer time at the truck for me and then give up. I wouldn't have lasted more than ten days with the supplies I had, but I got lucky and found a forestry cabin with some canned goods. That sustained me for fifteen more days. Then I packed up and headed back to civilization."

"Did you know where you were?"

"I'm *still* not sure. On my way down I remember seeing a place where all the trees are gnarled into grotesque shapes, I guess from the wind. It was blowing like a tornado up there."

"That's Two-Top," Lara said. "Did you find a road there?"

"Yeah. I followed it down through Big Springs and onto the main highway, and that's where I ran into you." Steve took her chin in his hand. "Then I grew a little lax. I should have been working harder to find them and their money, but...a certain woman stepped back into my life and I figured I'd have a bit of time before they were comfortable moving a stash so big. Especially with me still at large." A small grin appeared on his face. "At least I thought up a great escape route."

He reminded Lara of a little boy telling his mommy he'd learned to tie his shoes, but his actions made her furious. "I can't believe you purposely jumped into the spillway. You could have been killed!"

"Well, hell, Lara, I was going to die if they caught me. I figured I'd rather off myself than give those jerks the satisfaction."

She stared at him, her mood softened only a little by his grin. Then she said, "How was your ride down the spillway? I've always wondered what it would be like."

Steve shuddered. "Better and worse than any waterslide in the world. I had to hold my breath the entire time, and the force was incredible. It was like being tumbled in a giant washing machine! When it shot me out the mouth of Box Canyon, I felt like I was blasted from a cannon. It was all I could do to swim back to shallow water. The whole ordeal only took a matter of minutes, but it seemed like a lifetime. I laid in the water for a while before I could get my legs working again, and then I started the long crawl up the side of that damn steep mountain. There were times that the only thing keeping me from falling back into the river were the tree trunks."

"Tell me about it," Lara said. Remembering her fall made her wince with pain, but that decided her on something else. "I've laid here long enough. Every joint is killing me. I've got to move around before my limbs petrify."

Steve helped her to a sitting position. As he did, a surge of heat shot up her spine.

"I've definitely bruised my tailbone," she said through clenched teeth. "Help me stand. I can't bear to sit."

Standing relieved the pressure from her back but did nothing for the renewed throbbing in her ankle. She couldn't put any weight on it, and the only comfort she could get was lying down again.

Steve shook his head sadly. "I'm so sorry, Lara. I would never intentionally hurt you."

Tears gathered in the corners of his eyes, and Lara's breath caught in her chest at the display of unguarded emotion. His gaze searched hers, the irises darkening to a deeper shade of green.

"I know that, Steve," she said. "And I would never intentionally hurt you either. I never *ever* meant to."

She reached a hand to his rough cheek, and his dark head bent down so he could claim her lips with his own. The kiss was as delicate as the call of a distant meadowlark. Lara felt cherished, loved, and protected, and the trouble they were in seemed very far away. She also knew the peace wouldn't last.

Chapter Seventeen

With Steve's help, Lara's rehabilitation slowly progressed. Her condition made it impossible for them to leave the shack, but by the second day he felt confident the detectives hadn't followed her.

Maybe this was the safest place to be right now, but it wouldn't last forever. The problem was getting her down the mountain and back to safety. He knew she wouldn't be able to walk for a few days. Steve didn't have a cell phone because they were too easy to track, and Lara had left hers behind as well. She told him she doubted there would be reception. She'd also warned Jan and her uncle not to come looking for them for at least a week.

"I've come to a decision," he said while carving her a new pair of crutches with his pocketknife. Their renewed relationship had healed him, made him stronger and readier to face danger. "I'm going to get this damn mess over with once and for all. I refuse to go on living like I'm the criminal. Those bastards have been in charge of the situation long enough."

Lara's question was a whisper. "What? What are you planning?"

Steve stopped mid-stroke. He looked at the face he loved more than breathing, and a lump formed in his throat at the hesitancy of her question. Most of the time she was a firebrand, a strong woman with a mind of her own, but occasionally she slipped into an expression of helplessness, of childlike innocence. Both sides of her nature were adorable.

He set down his knife and the crutch and lay beside her. Gently wrapping his arms around her, he cradled her like the sweet child she seemed and comforted her like a loving parent. "First? I'm going for help. You need to get to a hospital."

She stared at him with those beautiful brown eyes, and he had a strong urge to make love to her over and over again. He didn't give in, though. She was too broken and hurting.

"I love you, Lara. You've put on a brave front, but I know you're in a lot of pain and I can't stand to see you like this anymore. Not even to protect me. We need to get you help. I've also got a life to live, and I'm not going to live it looking over my shoulder."

She put her head down and snuggled closer to his chest. The gesture warmed him and reminded him of everything that he'd be fighting for. An unseen force had brought them back together, and he knew it was for a reason: They were meant to be together for as long as they lived. His job now was to make sure they both lived a very long time.

She looked up, and he watched a crystal tear glide down her cheek.

"What?" he asked tenderly. "Tears now? You didn't cry when I hit you over the head."

"I don't cry when I'm mad," she said. "Only when I'm happy."

Steve pulled her close, and he kissed her with the passion of a free man, free from the boundaries that his own heart had set up over the past fifteen years. Lara loved him. She loved still, and she always had. That made everything okay, even a world full of corruption and vice. He was free now to love her wholly, without constraint or restraint. They were truly meant to be together.

He wanted to drink in the nearness of her, and forgetting everything but his hunger he made to roll atop Lara. Her slight gasp of pain brought him back to reality.

"Are you okay, honey?" He took a ragged breath. "I'm so sorry. What can I do to make you more comfortable?"

God, he couldn't bear the thought of her being hurt, especially not by him, not even by accident. He wanted to be her protection from now until the end of time, wanted to shield her and grant her every single wish she ever made. And now they had a chance for him to do just that.

* * *

Perhaps the situation was a boon, Lara decided. With the question of sex completely out of the way for a few days, her relationship with

Steve changed. The two talked, slipping easily into a comfort zone that only true friends share, where neither has to weigh words but speaks openly and never with rancor. It was better even than when they'd been kids.

Lara treasured each changing moment. She knew Steve felt the same. Fresh, honest laughter resounded through the tiny cabin. At other times, comfortable silence suited their purpose. Subjects from science to politics seemed to come up, and they both answered honestly, guilelessly, the topics explored and then neatly folded and put away. They covered a lot of ground, sometimes digging up emotional baggage but then burying it again with a splendid eulogy. Their scattered insecurities slowly molded into one powerful bond.

With history put to rest, they both enjoyed a great serenity. They knew perfectly where each other had been, how they'd got there, and who they were striving to become. They discussed the core of their growing relationship, too, insight of where they both believed their love could take them. Then they set aside the crisis at hand and made plans for the future.

Lara just hoped they'd make it to that future.

If only she weren't injured.

She shifted to a more suitable position, her emotions too close to the surface for her to speak. Steve's sudden desire surprised her, but it wasn't unwelcome. Something had been released inside of him, some kind of primitive strength. She longed to experience it full-force, have it race through her being. She wanted Steve to fill up the last cold corners of her heart and erase all the ridicule Philip had pumped inside her.

She knew he could do it. When they'd made love he was ardent, but he was also kind and caring. This time his kiss alone had melted her body. And they were alone here. But while her mind needed him, her body betrayed her. She hurt beyond belief—and hadn't bathed for three days! She wondered why this never happened in the novels she read. Those women were always clean, fit, and ready.

"Could I have a couple of pain relievers?"

She had brought a small bottle in case Steve needed them. She never dreamed she'd use the whole bottle herself.

Steve held up her head while she took the pills and drank from the canteen. As she lay back down, however, he straddled her in one lithe movement. He held himself above her, adding no pressure to her body, and teasingly kissed the tip of her nose. Then he nibbled on her ears, first one then the other; and then with feather-light kisses he touched each corner of her mouth.

"I want desperately to make love to you," he confessed. "But I know it's out of the question." He brushed his rough cheek against her smooth one. "Yet...if I've got to bear this torture, I'm going to make you suffer a little too. If we could do it once, we can do this much again."

Swiftly he unbuttoned her flannel shirt and tugged at her sports bra. His hand reached around her back for a clasp of the tight-fitting garment, and Lara suppressed a giggle as a puzzled look crossed his face. Apparently it was a good thing she'd taken it off herself the last time they hooked up.

"Damn, what *is* this thing you're wearing?"

Lara laughed. "It's my protection from your sweet torture."

"Oh yeah? Well, I've broken tougher cases than this. Let's see...," he said mysteriously. Then, "I think I can get the reaction I'm looking for without removal."

His lips pressed down on hers. One hand supported his weight while the other brushed back and forth against her nipple. When it stood out, dark and erect through the white cotton fabric of her bra, he smiled down at her and twirled an imaginary handlebar mustache. "You see what I mean, my sweet?"

Lara groaned softly, as he'd gone to work on the other breast and her pain was suddenly replaced with a sweeter kind of discomfort. She arched her back to give him better access, wishing that she hadn't worn a bra at all.

Instead of pulling the garment up, Steve chose to focus on her lips. He kissed Lara with renewed relish, and it was even better than before. Forgetting her injuries, Lara twisted her body to cuddle in closer...but her back refused to accept what her heart desired. Clenching her teeth, she gasped in pain.

Steve's green eyes stared down into hers. He wore a dazed expression, as if he'd just awakened from a dream, then his earlier playfulness became a much more earnest intent and he shook his head as if to clear the cobwebs.

"I'm taking this way too seriously. I gotta get some air."

With one quick push he was off of her and out the door, but not before Lara noticed that his discomfort was as great or greater than her own.

Chapter Eighteen

The following day Lara learned to use the crutches Steve made her. She was getting around much easier, the bump on her head had disappeared, and Steve made a natural concoction of herbs and rubbed the paste into her back, making her tailbone feel much better. "You really did learn a few things in your Boy Scout years, didn't you?"

"Oh, you have no idea, sweetheart. And wait until you're well again. I'll show you a few tricks I've learned since." His gorgeous grin was twisted with an evil gleam.

She hobbled over to where he was stirring soup from a package. That delicacy had accounted for their last few meals.

"What are you serving for dinner, James?" she asked in a very proper English accent.

"Beef Wellington, my lady. I hope you'll find it to your liking."

Steve's terrible accent made Lara laugh, but she was soon quieted by the serious expression on his face.

"Lara, I've *got* to go for help tomorrow. This is the last of the food, and we're out of water."

Lara shook her head. "I'm not letting you go down that mountain without me, Steve. McKay and Johnson could be waiting."

"You can't walk that far and you know it," he said. "I know you've been healing, but…well, the terrain is so rugged up here we wouldn't make a mile with you in a wheelchair let alone those primitive crutches."

She'd known this would happen. Lara had tried to prepare herself, but Scarlett Syndrome had taken over. *I'll think about it tomorrow* had become her mantra. Apparently tomorrow was here.

"I've been thinking about it, Steve. I know a way that is less wooded and steep. It's a lot longer than the way we came, but your chances of meeting a fisherman or hiker are better. If you could find someone, maybe *they* could go for help."

"Ah," Steve said as he poured some instant soup for her. He sounded relieved that she was going to let him go. "That sounds like a good plan. Come on, your Beef Wellington is getting cold."

They ate and then got into their sleeping bags, lay cradled in each other's arms. Kisses were gentle, touches tender, words whispered barely louder than the sounds of the swaying pines. The world below this mountain, Lara believed, wouldn't understand what they had shared in the last few days. It wasn't about sex at all— though she was looking forward to the day they could get back to that.

To be honest, she was afraid of going home. She was fearful of what the future might take from the serenity she and Steve had found here. But she also believed they could do even better. The future was terrifying, but it was also exhilarating. And she could always come back to this time in her mind, shut her eyes and cherish the memory.

Steve brushed wisps of her hair from her brow with his lips and then proved they were perfect for each other. "We have connected, my love, in a way I never dreamed possible. Beyond sex, beyond simple emotion... I can't explain it."

Lara just nodded and snuggled closer.

"Hey," Steve said. "Remember back in high school, the night we ran out of gas twenty-five miles out of town? We were juniors. You were so afraid—of the night noises and that your dad was going to ground you for life. That he would never let me see you again."

Lara gave a quiet chuckle. "I remember it was early October and cold. You gave me your letterman jacket and you only had a tee-shirt on underneath. I also recall that you weren't afraid of anything. You made fun of me when that owl let out a long 'hoooo' and I nearly peed my pants."

"Yeah." Steve paused. "Speaking of that...I also remember that I told you I had to stop to pee, and you were so mad. What was with that?"

"You really don't know?"

"No. I walked away from you and turned my back!"

Lara laughed. "It was because I needed to go so bad my eyes were swimming, but I was a proper lady and wouldn't dream of telling you that I needed to go squat in the weeds for a minute. There you were, simply walking off to take care of business!"

Steve shook his head, grinning. "God, girls are so dumb sometimes."

"And you sound twelve years old."

Steve leaned back and looked her in the eye. "No, I'm serious. Men don't worry about having to pee or fart or burp. We just let nature take its course. It's the plight of every woman to try to change all natural things."

She looked right back at him. "There's a fine line between 'changing natural things' and being polite."

He laughed. "Maybe so."After a moment he sobered. "You're going to be alone while I'm gone. If you're scared—"

She cut him off, raising her chin in the air. "Stop right there, Steve Mitchell. I want you to know right now that I'm over all of that. *All* of it. I'm not afraid of the dark, I'm perfectly fine on my own, and I've spent the majority of the last fifteen years in the woods with all the scary animals. So you won't have to worry about me. I can take care of myself."

"Yeah," Steve said, clearly razzing her. "I can see how well you do on your own. A bump on your head, a broken tailbone and a sprained ankle? You're doing just fine!"

She punched him. "Two out of the three of these injuries *you* gave me, so stay clear, buddy, and watch your back. Paybacks are a bitch where I come from."

Steve just grinned. "I feel like I need to tell you how I feel about you over and over again before I leave in the morning. I want to tell you how you've refilled my life with love and laughter and hope."

Lara embraced him. "You don't need to, Steve. I know. And I feel the same. I'm in a place I've never been before. My soul knows pure contentment."

He leaned back to look at her. "Do you believe in fate, Lara?"

She was silent a few moments before answering. "I don't know if 'fate' is the right word, but I believe that God can direct us when we listen. And I honestly believe that He had a hand in bringing you back to me. And I'm grateful."

"Yes," Steve said simply.

Lara continued, reminding herself of the fact as much as him. "I can't imagine that He would take you from me now. He is not cruel."

"No, He isn't. I see that now. The world is a dark place, but there's light too. So we have to believe that the next few days will somehow work out to our advantage."

"I love you, Steve."

"And I, you."

Their kiss was beyond tender. Then they slept.

Chapter Nineteen

Steve checked his pack once more before strapping it onto his back. He worked quickly, his head lowered. It was time to go. The sooner he left, the faster he could get help and return. He'd packed light, leaving almost everything except his gun.

Concern was etched on Lara's features. "Steve, remember what I told you last night. Don't take any crazy chances. McKay and Johnson must be waiting somewhere down there. First and foremost, protect yourself. I'll be fine."

"I'll get help and be back as soon as possible."

She moved in front of him, leaning on her crutches. "You make sure you stay alive." She reached up and touched his cheek, which was rugged from his lack of shaving. "Without you, life will cease to exist for me."

Steve took her by the shoulders, feeling a similar nervousness now that they were outside of their sleeping bag cocoon and he was headed back down into danger. "Stop that. You're being melodramatic. Of course life would go on without me. It would have to. You are a beautiful person and you've worked hard to get where you are. If something happens…well, don't squander that. No matter what, you must promise me that you'll go on living your dreams. *Our* dreams." He pulled her against him. "I can finally say that again. So, please, you have to promise me."

The expression in Lara's eyes was as if someone had knocked her to the floor. "Stay, Steve. Lawrence and Jan will come looking for us in a couple of days and—"

He shook his head. "We're almost out of water, Lara. You only have a half a cup to last until I get back. This is the only way." He kissed her one last time. "I love you. Let's believe that will get us through. And, well, thank you for loving me back."

134

He extricated himself then and walked out into the pale morning light. Behind him, Lara wept openly, leaning on the door with the crooked hinges. He would keep that memory on the whole way down the mountain.

* * *

The morning dragged on like a bad dream. The sun was thin and high, even from her elevated perch, and Lara had felt the last of her energy seep from her body as Steve's silhouette disappeared over the crest of the hill to the west.

She hopped further outside without the aid of her crutches and leaned back against the rotting wall of the shack. She had always found great comfort in these mountains, a personal strength that she'd never felt anywhere else, but today was different. There was the possibility Steve would die in the forest, gunned down by the men who'd chased him for weeks. If that happened, she'd die too. Of course, that would be for the best. She truly believed that a benevolent God would let them be together again in a better world.

Lara smiled weakly at the thought. Steve would call her melodramatic again if she voiced her thoughts, but they shared a pure love that could conquer death. They'd already defeated the mistakes of their past.

"That's still what I believe," she said out loud, imagining that Steve could hear her with his heart. "But you must live, dammit. You must."

After an hour of praying and fantasizing about a future with Steve, Lara hopped on her good leg back into the shack. She grabbed two pieces of Jan's homemade smoked jerky, the strong aroma of which made her stomach growl, then hopped again out into the morning sunshine. As she did, from the corner of her eye Lara noticed two large birds winging their way toward the reservoir.

They were life-mating cranes. Was that a sign? She decided it was.

Slightly comforted, leaning against the shack she slid to the ground in a half sitting, half lying position, and she took a nap in the morning sunshine. When she woke, it looked and felt like noon. The sun blazed down from directly above her. Steve had been gone several hours.

She shook her head, trying to clear it, and her agitation returned. She tried to recall what had woken her. A…a noise of some kind?

There it was again.

Lara held very still and listened intently. It was something in the willows to her left, and her injuries kept her from moving quickly or quietly back into the shack. Was it the detectives? Had they found Steve? Had they killed him? Had they passed him on the mountain but would now finish her off instead?

A gangly baby moose stepped out into the clearing. His knees bulged, giving him a comical gait on skinny bowed legs. He pulled leaves and mountain huckleberries into his mouth, and Lara grinned as she watched, wishing she'd brought a camera. She also held very still. If she made any movement, the calf would be long gone.

To her left a loud snort rang out, and Lara turned to see the baby's mother appear around the corner of the shed. She froze, trying not to blink or breathe. *What a dumbass,* she berated herself. She of all people knew better than to expect a baby moose to be far from her mother, and there was nothing worse than getting between a mama and her calf. Moose were extremely protective and dangerous when it came to defending their young. Fisherman and tourists were attacked every year in that sort of situation. In fact, not a week ago she'd seen a YouTube video of a man in Yellowstone damn near trampled to death.

This mother stood less than two feet away, looking right down her long snout at Lara.

Lara stared back, frozen in terror. The beast was at least seven and a half feet tall and it easily weighed a thousand pounds. Lara had no barrier she could hide behind, and she would have no chance of running with her injuries.

Well, moose had very poor eyesight. She knew that was her best and only hope. Of course, their noses made up for the lack, and Lara not only had a human smell but a piece of jerky in her pocket. Not that the moose would want to eat the jerky, being a vegetarian and all, but she would definitely smell something funny.

Oh. Actually she'd been kind of stupid to step outside with the jerky at all. If a bear had smelled it, Lara would be in even bigger trouble.

Ugh. She needed to breathe. She didn't think she could hold still much longer, either, so she tried to take the tiniest of breaths while staring directly at the overbearing moose. She tried not to move more than necessary.

The mother leaned close and swished her nose against Lara's hair, turned and looked toward her baby. Lara stayed frozen, and that seemed to work. Without another glance the moose sauntered over to her offspring and the two started eating alongside each other.

Lara rolled slowly back inside the shack, and as quickly and quietly as possible she pushed the door shut with her good foot. The hinges made a creaking noise, and a moment later she heard both moose lope away.

"Holy shit!" she said out loud. She was safe.

An hour later she was still shaking when she heard the sound of four-wheelers coming her way.

Was it the bad guys?

Lara only suffered a few moments of terror before she heard Jan yelling her name. Realizing with relief that she wouldn't have to spend a night alone in the wilderness, she slumped over against the cabin wall. Somehow Steve had made it for help. Either that or Jan had come looking for her early. Either way, Lara sent a silent prayer of thanks to the heavens.

A few minutes later, Steve and her Uncle Lawrence were carefully lifting her into a type of sleigh on wheels. Lara tried to talk to them, but they shushed her and said there'd be time enough for explanations later.

The trip down the mountain on the padded toboggan turned out to be the worst pain Lara could imagine. However, by nine o'clock that evening Lara's ankle had been cast, she'd had x-rays of her back, she'd had a shower and downed a couple of Oxytocin.

Clean and comfortable, resting in her own bed, she heard Jan fussing downstairs in the kitchen. Uncle Lawrence was there, too; she heard him whistling while building a fire. She hadn't let Steve leave her side. She was so relieved and thrilled that he was safe, she didn't want him out of her sight. But she did want to know how exactly he'd found Uncle Lawrence and Jan, so she called down to them and made her uncle come up.

Lawrence sat in an oversized chair in her loft that looked over the great room and down to the Buffalo River outside. "We were already on our way," he began. "We came alone, so we wanted to move quick. We didn't include the search-and-rescue team because the men after Steve were handing out hundreds to anyone willing to give them information. Jan and I don't think anyone would say anything, but…well, better safe than sorry. Just in case anyone else has figured out that you two are in love. By the way, Steve, welcome to the family."

Steve accepted the older man's outstretched hand.

Lawrence raised his head and really looked at Steve, who turned to Lara and grinned.

Lawrence. He was as sharp as they came. And Steve… Well, she loved both of her men, and if they could just get through this mess the two men would be best friends.

Her uncle continued. "The thugs have left town for a couple of days. That's why we decided it was safe to come up. Unfortunately, they plan on returning Saturday. They're visiting their law enforcement contacts and seeing what they can find out about any prosecution." He glanced at Steve. "I hope your people are keeping everything hushed."

"How do you know all this?" Lara asked in astonishment.

"I told you we bugged their rooms, but we also did their rental car. I had one of my friends follow them to Idaho Falls airport just to be sure they got on the plane." Lawrence glanced at Steve again. He looked as proud as a papa holding his firstborn.

"Thank you again, sir," Steve said, stretching out to shake Lara's uncle's hand. "I'm impressed at the way you've helped."

Lawrence shrugged. "I have my own equipment and I know some good people. We have a lot of transients come to Island Park, so we've learned over the years to keep an eye out for anything suspicious. Quietly."

"Okay everybody, soup's on!" shouted Jan from below. "Lawrence, you and Steve come and help me, and we'll take supper upstairs."

Both men hurried down, and within minutes Lara's round antique table that she used for a desk and fly-tying was cleared and covered with a tablecloth. Wine, homemade bread and butter, and an ivory crock full of beef stew were placed in its middle. Jan had the men bring up three folding chairs while she prepared everything Lara would need on a tray.

"Now," Jan commanded, "before we go one step further with eating or making plans for the upcoming days, we are going to have a prayer and I'm saying it." She bowed her head, as did Lara and the two men in her life. Lara was somewhat surprised. She hadn't known until tonight that her friend shared in her faith.

"Dear God, we are so thankful that you have answered our prayers this day, that you have brought our family back to us against the odds we now face. We ask you to bless this food and continue to protect us throughout the coming days of this trial. Amen."

They all repeated the "Amen," and Lara sat looking at the people she loved most in the world. She thought her heart might break. She had been very moved by Jan's prayer, and she was still moved by the good fortune she'd received through the last few weeks. No matter the difficulties they faced, she had Steve back and she had two people who loved her more than anything.

Jan's stew was a welcome relief after the watery soups they'd eaten on the mountain. It was hearty, with rich brown gravy, carrots, potatoes, onions, and thick chunks of tender beef. The bites of bread and butter melted in Lara's mouth, and her desire for more made it difficult not to talk with her mouth full.

"I think I've died and gone to heaven, Jan! That bread is so delicious. My belly is growling for more. Why didn't you ever cook like this for me before? Just leaning on your fancy out-of-town chef?"

"I'm starting on my second bowl," Steve piped up. "I've never had a better meal in my life. Even after hitchhiking for about three days, I never imagined food could taste this good. And I was *starving*."

Lawrence took a sip of wine, and Lara recognized the look in his eye. He was about to impart some trivia tidbit, which was a habit when he was with friends and felt comfortable. "Speaking of that... I was reading in one of my Old West magazines the other day about the origin of the term 'hitchhiking.' It seems it was common practice in the olden days to use one horse for two people. One person would ride the horse from points A to B and the other guy would walk. Then the second guy would get on the horse and ride from B to C. After that, they'd both walk alongside the horse from C to D and let him rest. Then they would start over again. That's how they named it 'hitching a ride.' Then, later, when cars were invented, they changed it to hitchhiking."

"That's interesting," Steve remarked. Then he laughed. "I've never even thought about how that term came to be."

Lara grinned. "Oh, my dear uncle knows more off-the-wall trivia than you can imagine. Never play Trivial Pursuit with him—unless he's on your team." She gave Lawrence a loving look.

"I'll have to remember that," Steve said. "And I hope we get the chance to play sometime soon."

The comment brought silence along with a renewed sense of their current reality. Steve apparently wasn't ready to talk strategy, so he changed the subject back to food.

"This stew is incredible, Jan. When did you have time to make this?"

"I cooked every minute you two were gone. It's a nervous habit. I've got enough meals in the freezer to feed the four of us until Christmas!"

Lara couldn't stand it any longer. They had to deal with the bad guys. "Uncle Lawrence," she spoke up. "What else do you know about those two crooks following Steve?"

"Apparently they followed Steve at the reservoir with my boat. It was next to Jan's. They were sure Steve was in it when it went over the side, but when they got down there, nobody was around. No body, no tracks. Then Ol' Man Jacobs reported Jan's boat had wrecked into his dock another mile up the reservoir."

"I'll get you a new boat, Jan," Steve said. "Sorry about that."

"That old heap wasn't worth much," the woman said, "but I'll let you buy me a good used one to replace it."

Lara's uncle continued. "They spent the next two days looking in the water and questioning people in the homes on Bill's Island." He glanced over at Lara. "From what I can tell, they don't have a clue that you're involved. They know there's a girl, but they still haven't got a name."

"Thank God," Steve said, "I want to keep it that way. Thank you, sir. I really can't tell you what it means to me to have people like you willing to help a man they hardly know."

"Quit calling me 'sir.' You make me feel like an old duffer!" Lawrence grinned, but his next words were low and serious. "They want you dead, son."

Lara's heart stopped beating in her chest. She'd already known what her uncle said to be true, but hearing confirmation from him was almost more than she could bear.

"Why wouldn't they just figure you were dead and go about their business?" Jan asked Steve.

"When over four million dollars is at risk, you don't assume anything until it's proven. That's why Lara is still in danger."

"What are we going to do, Steve?"

"*We* aren't going to do anything," he told her sternly. The steeliness was back in his eyes. "The first thing I'm going to do is get away from here so that you three are safe." He hurried on, seeing her indignation. "You've done all that you can, honey. I want you out of the way so I don't have to worry about you."

"Out of the way?" she repeated. "Out of the way! How dare you?"

Jan and Lawrence sat quiet, but Steve's volume matched her own. "I'll tell you how I dare, damn it! You mean too much to me to involve you further. I've got to finish this myself. I'll come back as soon as this mess is cleaned up."

Lara shook her head. "Look, Steve Mitchell, I waited fifteen years for you to come back to me. You almost took me out of the game when I came up the mountain, but I lived through hell week with you there and am only more resolved. If you think that now the game's in overtime you can shut me in the locker room, you're sadly mistaken! I'm in, coach, like it or not!"

She stared at Steve, hoping she had persuaded him. When she only saw determination on his rugged face, she tried a different tack, an appeal to his heart. "Damn it, Steve. You can't leave now that we've found each other again. I just can't bear it."

Jan and Lawrence sat still, but Steve walked over and sat on the edge of her bed. "And I couldn't bear it if you got hurt because of me. You can't help me all banged up like you are. I promise you, my love, I will take every available precaution. I have more to live for now than ever in the past. I love you. You are the most important thing in my life. But if we are ever to have a future together, we are going to have to get this mess behind us once and for all. I don't want to live the rest of my life looking over my shoulder. Now, get some rest," he demanded, touching her cheek. "I'm going to finalize some plans, and then I'll be back to sleep by your side tonight. Okay?"

Lara nodded. He was right that she couldn't move around enough to help him as she was, but that didn't change the fact that she *wanted* to. She had tears in her eyes and couldn't speak, but maybe there was nothing more to be said.

At least they knew they loved each other. That was something.

Steve and the others got up and left, taking the dinner dishes. Lara half dozed, wanting to heal, wanting to be helpful. There was no way the ankle would be fixed by the time the detectives got back, however. She was out of the game.

She was still agitated when Steve returned, but he seemed unfazed and his eyes never left hers as he undressed. He had always been steadfast, which was one of the many reasons she loved him. Looking at him rekindled that same deep yearning in her that had been building for the last few days.

He crawled into bed and cuddled up next to her, forgetting her cast until his leg hit its rough surface. He threw back the covers, exposing the bright purple cast, and said, "Ha! Just as I expected. She has girded herself for battle. Never fear, however. I shall overcome."

She laughed. "What are you going to do, my hero, take off my cast?"

"Nae, lassie," he said in a perfect Scottish accent, clearly having noticed the Highlander romances on her bookshelf. "But I can help the situation. Your wee little toes look so sad sticking out of that cold hard plaster, I think I'll warm them up."

Lara settled back on her pillows, expecting a warm sock to be pulled over her foot. Instead, she jumped in surprise as Steve's wet tongue touched her big toe.

"This little piggy went to market…"

His words were muffled as he devoured her big toe, and Lara felt a sensual electricity surge through her foot, moving up her leg and settling somewhere below her tummy. Steve continued, favoring each toe with the same intimate attention, all the while murmuring unintelligible messages.

"Steve, *stop,* " she heard herself moan, but the protest was weak to say the least.

He continued with her other foot, nipping at her trembling flesh. She felt silly and embarrassed, as if he were doing something totally unethical. And yet, when she stopped to think about it, wasn't this act much less intimate than having sex? This seemed…so much more. But Lara finally succumbed to the erotic pleasure.

When the last toe was reasonable satisfied, Steve kissed her ankle, her calf, the back of her knee—places she'd never dreamed could be erogenous zones. He reached the inside of her thigh, but he teasingly switched to the other leg and traveled back down. By the time he reached her cast, Lara arched to have more of his attention higher up.

He abruptly changed position. Turning up her palm, he began nibbling at each fingertip before taking the finger in his mouth and sucking lingeringly. He licked her wrist, leaving a wet trail to the inside curve of her elbow and beyond to her shoulder. The passion mounted in Lara. She thought she'd die.

Steve's desire had become more evident as well. She felt him through his black briefs, harder than stone, pushing against her thigh. His light kisses changed to delicate bites and nibbles on her shoulder, neck and ear, and his breath churned heavily in that broad chest. Lara reached out and heard him groan as she stroked his head, while with her other hand she rubbed his back and buttocks, memorizing each curve and contour.

Steve's mouth finally moved to her breast, which felt heavy with passion and the need to be touched, licked, and sucked by this man. He quickly did all three when she threw her nightgown over her head and to the floor.

Lara's body needed release. Her flesh demanded an orgasm, commanded her to take Steve's love deep inside of her, so she pushed him slightly away then guided him back and into her throbbing womanhood. Damn the distant pain in her tailbone; she was going to have this man explode inside of her and soon.

Very, very soon.

She watched his eyes glaze just before her own need made all vision smoky and unfocused. Her breath came in soft, jerking pauses, her body growing impossibly more attuned to the pleasure of his inside her. Lara's lips touched his ear, and she whispered fevered words of lust, commanding Steve to take her slower and gentler. She wanted to experience the oneness she had only read about: the coming of two at once, the union of souls.

His reaction was just as she expected, just as she desired. The pulse of their passion consumed them both. His cadence intensified, and Steve took her to the highest place she'd ever been, to the mystical point that she'd dreamed about but never experienced. Now she knew *exactly* what was meant about that white heat stirring your soul and proving that lovemaking should never be taken for granted. It was truly a gift of heaven.

Done, lying in his arms, she marveled that two human beings so infinitely different could create such an extraordinary pleasure for one another. She had met her soul mate, the man who would love her mentally and physically forever, and now it would just get better and better. It was a sobering thought that she had almost thrown this away forever.

Steve did not seem to be thinking about the same thing. During the night, he brought her to that secret place of white heat again and again.

"Is this normal?" Lara asked in astonishment after her fourth orgasm.

"Babe," he said, slowly shaking his head. "Nothing has ever been 'normal' with you, and I have a strong feeling that's it's never going to be."

"Is that a bad thing?" she asked.

"It is the best thing in the world," he said with a sly grin.

Chapter Twenty

The next morning Lawrence arrived bright and early. "I've had a chance to listen to the most recent tape from the bug I hid in McKay and Johnson's rooms," he stated without preamble.

Lara and Steve looked at each other and back at Lara's uncle.

"McKay told Johnson that he knows the Snake River like the back of his hand. He's been bragging that he knows 'the point of no return' at the falls. That's where the money is, because I heard Johnson 'will have to maintain the canoe while McKay gets *the package* from the far side'—right at the 'point of no return.'"

"'The package,'" Steve repeated. "Does anyone ever go out to that area to camp, or is there a road of any kind?"

"No, not on that side of the river. You have to drive on the left side of the road and cross the water. The only way to get to that spot is by boat." Lawrence gave him a pointed look. "But I don't know anyone crazy enough to get that close to the falls, let alone maneuver a canoe or raft around to stash money there. McKay must be a crazy damn psycho to even try. And I doubt Johnson knows how dangerous those falls are. No one's ever gone over the edge and lived."

Steve shook his head. "Four million dollars does stupid things to people."

"The area is so remote that a bag of money could be sitting behind a tree and no one would ever see it," Lawrence admitted. "And McKay thinks...well, he thinks that if you're still alive and following him he can get you to go over Mesa Falls to your death. And, well...they now also know the woman you've been seeing is Lara, and they plan to follow her for a couple of days to see if she can lead them to you."

Lawrence gave Lara a concerned look. So did Steve. When she shook her head, her uncle continued.

"They made another reservation for three days from now. McKay also called someone else. A female. He told her that he would be home for a couple of days and then come back here. He told whomever he was talking to that in a few days they would have *everything.* Sounds like he doesn't expect to share with Johnson."

"Huh," Steve said. "There's no honor among thieves. Did he tell Johnson exactly where to keep the canoe once they're on the river?"

"Yes," Lawrence said. "There's a sign at Hatchery Ford that says, 'DANGEROUS WATERFALLS AHEAD. STOP AT THIS POINT FOR YOUR SAFETY.' There used to be a closer sign, but the current wiped it out and it was never replaced. At that spot, there are some buoys with ropes across the water, but depending on the water flow they can be almost completely submerged. Still, they're bright orange, and you can see something is different in the river there."

"Those ropes are probably how he got the money to the far side. McKay is a big man—six-five or six-six, and he's got to weigh close to two-seventy-five."

Lawrence nodded. "He looks closer to three hundred pounds now, but that river is mean and ugly. He probably thinks he's big and strong enough to fight that current, but I doubt there's a human alive that can, at least not the way the water's acting recently. If he really did leave the money there, he better have studied every rock and hole for a long time to know exactly how to manage while holding his loot."

"I'll bet he's had this hiding place dreamed up for years," Steve muttered.

Lawrence nodded. "Since his family's been coming up here for a long time…yeah. This could have been one of those D.B. Cooper things, never solved."

Steve grunted. "Apparently McKay's not stupid. Just corrupt." Still, now that he knew McKay and Johnson's plans, for the first time ever he felt he had the upper hand.

Lawrence went back to the TroutHunter.

"Steve, what is our next step?" Lara asked in a shaky voice.

"The first thing I need to do is call my supervisor at the FBI. I've been in contact with him once since I got to Island Park, because until I had a better idea of where the money might be there was nothing he could do without possibly alerting them. Now there is."

He picked up his phone and went out on the deck. When he reentered the kitchen, Lara asked, "What did he say?"

"He's got some phone calls to make, but he said he's sure he can get me the help I need. It seems these two have gotten away with similar crimes before, and some of that's coming to light. A lot of people we thought were McKay and Johnson's 'friends' are now backing away."

"Are you kidding?" Lara said. "They've gotten away with this before?"

"Yes, but on a much smaller scale, thank goodness. It's not as easy as it sounds. That said, this kind of money is hard to live without once you've had a taste. Also…once you've tangled with the big boys, you're either in or dead. Driggs told me to work on my plan from this end and he'll call me back within a couple of hours. Will you check the Internet for an updated weather report, please? It may be a factor in my plan."

She stared at him. "Okay, Steve. But what exactly *is* your plan?"

He smiled sheepishly. "I haven't got one yet."

* * *

Lara and Steve had moved out into the morning sun. She saw him look up through the pines at a cloudless sky and then shake his head. "I don't understand how it can be so perfect today and tomorrow it's supposed to be twenty degrees colder and rainy."

Lara sipped her chamomile tea. "It happens all the time in Island Park. I've been on the river with clients when the temperature is seventy degrees one minute and fifteen degrees cooler ten minutes later. This is high country. Did you notice Sawtelle Peak? It snowed there two days ago."

Steve turned and gazed at the jutting crown majestically watching over the valley below, the tallest mountain in the area. "What's the elevation?"

"Over eleven thousand feet above timberline."

Steve stared. For several minutes he was silent, and then he took another gulp of his coffee. "I wanted to take you up there to see the wildflowers. Is the road safe to travel?"

Lara shrugged. "It's a pretty good dirt road, although they're switchbacks all the way to the top."

Steve didn't comment. Then he said, "We have a little time before McKay and Johnson come back. Do you want to...? You know, just in case. Maybe it'll help me think up a plan."

She looked at him and decided to stay positive. "Yes. It's a sweet idea. I haven't had a chance to go up there yet this year. The wildflowers are gorgeous. In fact, there are varieties that only grow in the highest parts of the area. Should we take a drive?"

Steve smiled. "I promised to help Jan this morning, and I'm supposed to sing later tonight, but I've got about three hours off this afternoon. Let's do it then."

"Sure," Lara said, grinning. "Let's."

Steve suddenly glanced down at the way she was sitting and seemed to have misgivings. "Are you sure you feel up to it? A dirt road with lots of switchbacks might be kind of rough on a bruised tailbone and a broken ankle in a cast."

Lara shrugged. "I'll take a pain pill just before we leave. Can you drive?"

"Yes," Steve said, getting to his feet. He walked to Lara's side and kissed her on the forehead. "Gladly. I've been wanting to do this with you for a long time now, and...well, there's no time like the present." He paused, and they both thought about the coming showdown with McKay and Johnson. He finished by saying, "I'll have Jan make us a couple of sandwiches so we can have a picnic on top. Sound good?"

"Perfect," Lara said.

"I'll be back for you at one o'clock."

Lara stayed in the morning sun watching the slow, tranquil water of the Buffalo River. This had been her favorite spot in the whole world until she'd found herself back in Steve's arms. Now she knew that she belonged with him no matter where that was.

Tomorrow. A shiver ran up her spine despite the warmness of the sun, and then she broke into a cold sweat. Though they hadn't said so, it was potentially their very last day together. She wanted to give Steve some options, perhaps some better ideas than the plan he'd already thought up and wouldn't tell her. He wouldn't tell her because with a broken ankle she would be of no help to him anyway—or so he thought.

Her teeth began to chatter as if she were in shock once again, and she pulled her crutches closer and hobbled back inside her cabin. She knew this country from one end to the other, so this was on her. This was the reason she and Steve had split up all those years ago, the reason she'd made that terrible mistake. It had all been so that she could come back here and figure out how to give the two of them a perfect life from here forward.

Well, that might be a little overboard, but they were back together again and nothing was going to take that away from her. She had four hours to figure out something that would save the love of her life, keep her safe, and put away the bad guys.

Chapter Twenty-One

The trip up the mountain was glorious. The afternoon air was balmy, and Lara had to agree with Steve's earlier statement that it seemed impossible tomorrow would be a dark, damp, day. The blue of the sky made it hard to imagine anything but sunshine.

Lara positioned her cast on the dashboard and lay back in her seat, ready to enjoy the utter beauty of the drive. She was determined to set her fears aside for a few hours and let the mountains comfort her as they had so many times in the past, and nature's abundance took her breath away as it always did. Her years of living here had not tarnished her amazement and devotion for the sights and sounds of Island Park. No number of years ever could.

She rolled down her window, inhaling the freshness of the countryside and pointing out the hidden treasures of the mountain while Steve drove slowly along the single-lane road. She spoke but never took her eyes from the spectacular view.

"The wildflowers are a little late because of last year's severe winter, but their profusion is unequaled."

The hills were covered in the blue-pod lupine, pink sticky geranium, white yarrow, goldenrod, and desert paintbrush that was a muted shade of orange. Under the Douglas firs lay hundreds of the blooms, looking as if a garden had been deliberately planted at the base of each; and quaking aspens stood side by side with the pines, as if there were no rules of discrimination in the forest, each living thing free to shine with its own unique splendor.

Steve slowed to a crawl as he took a particularly dangerous curve, and Lara looked up into a tall pine tree.

Something caught her eye.

"Oh, Steve, stop! There's something in that tree in front of us."

"Yeah, I saw it too," he agreed.

He drew the Jeep to a halt, and they watched a mother owl and her three babies, their beaks open as they screeched for food.

"That is amazing," Steve commented, considering her camouflage. "She looks just like the bark of a tree."

The owl turned her head completely around at that, as if she'd heard the comment and disapproved, and Lara bit back a laugh.

They traveled onward until Lara instructed Steve to turn the Jeep off the main road. The side path led into a richly dressed canyon in all shades of green, the floor of the ravine shrouded with thousands of flowers. It was a million times more impressive than what they'd seen on the way up.

"This is what would expect Heaven to look like," Steve murmured.

Lara felt a flush of pleasure, as this was yet another joy that they could share.

"Turn in here," she directed.

The dirt road curved slightly around the back of a hill and followed a crystal-clear stream filled with crisp watercress. Here, the road abruptly ended. Steve stopped the jeep and looked around. Lara just gazed at the secluded spot as if she were seeing the setting through Steve's eyes for the first time. The grass was waist deep. A gentle breeze stirred the tall blades. Quaking aspens with shimmering leaves were elegant roof over their heads.

Steve was quiet for a few moments, looking around him, and then he turned. "You brought me here with an ulterior motive, didn't you?"

Lara swung her cast from the jeep and slid onto the lush carpet of grass. "Get the blanket, honey. I'm starving."

"Me too," Steve said, and he looked her over from top to bottom.

That simple response was welcome—and necessary. He'd been right. She was planning on seducing him.

Which was *amazing,* she reflected. She felt confident enough in herself as a woman to dare do that now. It hadn't always been that way, especially after her youthful mistakes and the humiliation she suffered with Philip, and so she was amazed at the change. Her life was altered, and Steve was the reason; Steve, his willingness to forgive her, and her own willingness to forgive herself and move on.

"Steve," she whispered, "what are your plans for tomorrow?"

He eyed her. "I'm not sure yet. I've got some ideas, and I'm trying to work through them. I figured the drive down would give me more time to think, too."

They ate their picnic slowly. Lara enjoyed the serenity of simply being with the man she loved, of watching the way the sunlight changed his black hair to a shimmering navy blue. She adored the fact that she could reach over and touch his hand, or thigh, or cheek and have it feel as natural as breathing.

"This little place is amazing," Steve said. "One of the most beautiful settings I've ever seen."

Lara nodded, and her body was afire with tension. "I found this spot after my divorce. I knew it would be the perfect spot to make love, but…well, I honestly never thought I would find anyone to share it with. But now I've found you."

Steve put down his sandwich and took her hand.

"I was so…" She paused and took a deep breath. "So *damaged.* I couldn't even imagine the need to have sex again—ever. Can you imagine? Of course, until you made love to me I didn't even know how it was supposed to feel."

"Good?" Steve asked.

"Great," she replied. Then, "It's odd. You read about sex all the time and imagine it to be something beyond this world. After Phillip, I honestly believed that kind of intimacy didn't exist. Now I know how wrong I was. Now I could write my own book about the beauty of an intimate relationship, as I've seen what it can be—and what it will be."

Her emotions sometimes took complete control of her, so Lara tried to suppress any further outpouring. A moment later she saw a single tear slide down Steve's cheek and she knew she had nothing to worry about. She never would. She could share anything with this extraordinary man and he would always respect and worship her. Just as she did him.

"I love you, Steve," she whispered.

"And I love you, Lara."

He took her into his warm embrace, and the earth and sun bore witness as he laid her on their blanket and lingeringly removed each piece of clothing, kissing every inch of her body. Lara kept her eyes open except for the few times she said a silent prayer to God, thanking him for sending Steve back to her, for giving her a second chance. How few people received such a perfect gift?

Steve knelt above her and shed his clothing. There was no wide-eyed intensity this time, no lusty desperation, just an expression of the deepest admiration and respect. Lara had never felt so valued in her life, and it was surprisingly aphrodisiac. It was as if they'd crossed another threshold of unknown perfection.

"Thank you, Lara," Steve whispered, his voice soft as the fluttering leaves above. "Thank you for helping me believe in happy-ever-after."

Lara inhaled the heady aroma of the wildflowers, which were almost as intoxicating as Steve's words. This moment was perfect. She felt tears slipping down her cheeks, which Steve kissed away.

"I want to make love to you, Lara," he said. "I want to please you in every way imaginable."

She was so overcome that she could barely nod.

He was tender as any man ever loved a woman, and over the next hour he brought her to exquisite release over and over again before seeking his own pleasure. When that was accomplished, he lay down by her side on the blanket.

"Lara, for the first in a long time, I feel like I finally know what it is to love someone so much that her needs are more important than my own. After we split, I became hardened on the outside and cold. I don't blame you for that, but for awhile I was a selfish son of a bitch. I finally feel like myself again, and I have you to thank for some of my transformation."

They washed in the stream. Steve jumped right in, gasping at the cold. Lara, lying on the bank of the brook, giggled at the string of swearwords pouring from his mouth, but a moment later he was laughing at her in return as she tried to get her panties back on over her cast. Turnabout, it seemed was fair play.

Clothed again, they sat on the bank and stared at each other. Lara saw the doubt in his eyes. Then he looked away.

"Steve, look at me." Their eyes locked, and she imagined their two shades of green merging into one boiling cauldron of love and fear and hope. "This is *not* going to be our last day together. I swear it to you. Last night you said that you could see us together for a very long time. God wouldn't give us this second chance just to snatch it away from us, but it's our job to make sure that happens.

And since I know this whole area like the back of my hand, I've come up with an idea. I want you to listen carefully without comment until I'm finished."

She took a deep breath then and began to weave the details of her plan. There were as many twists and turns as the road Steve took to get them here, as many switchbacks as the Monaco Grand Prix. Then she explained that, no, she didn't know of anyone who had ever tried this, but she knew the river as well as anyone in Island Park. Better, maybe. She knew it so well that she could wander it in her sleep. Since childhood she had studied it, talked to it, and most importantly listened to it. She knew each stretch by the mile and landmark: a mountain with a small waterfall that trickled down a steep cliff and sprayed the rocks. A mountain that jutted out around a corner. The swift rapids past Harriman State Park. And last but not least, the place where every boat must get out of the water or go over the enormous Mesa Falls.

She spoke with confidence and authority, but secretly she had no idea if her plan would work. No one had ever attempted such a feat. But this, she was certain, was their best chance at a future.

* * *

Driggs, Steve's FBI supervisor, called when they were halfway back down the mountain. The reception was poor, so Steve promised to call him that evening. He was still thinking about Lara's idea, so now he could devote his entire attention to this incredible woman and trying to convince her that her plan was completely ludicrous.

"Okay, Lara. I heard everything you said, and some of it really makes sense. I think I can use bits and pieces. There's one thing, though... I refuse to let you get involved." He stopped her protest with his hand. "Now, listen to me. I heard you without interrupting, so now you hear me out."

Lara's mouth was a tight line, and Steve could see a muscle in her cheek clenching.

"Lara, you're hurt," he reminded her. "You have a big fat cast on your foot, and you walk like you're a hundred and three. I've got help coming. The FBI is more than equipped to handle any situation, and I'm certain they'll be here when I need them."

"Yeah, but—"

"Lara," Steve said, speaking slowly for effect. "Let me finish. Yes, you know this part of the Snake better than anyone around, but there is no way you can do everything you just suggested. Not as buggered up as you are. You know it."

"I don't know anything of the sort," she pouted, folding her arms.

He wanted to laugh. The fact that she was willing to put her life on the line for him was absolutely amazing, especially after the last fifteen years of anger and regret. He had never expected to be happy again, and he was deeply touched by all that she offered. But more than her willing sacrifice he wanted her alive, wanted her by his side for the rest of his life. And no matter the outcome of the mess was for him, he needed to keep Lara safe.

Lara of the old days would say it was time to pray. It didn't seem like a terrible idea.

Chapter Twenty-Two

Trouble. McKay and Johnson were back earlier than expected. Steve was just finishing his second set in the bar at Pond's Lodge when the two men he'd been after for over two months walked in. The pair took seats at a high table in the back of the room.

Steve was somewhat prepared, at least. Lawrence had called Jan right after the two detectives surprised him and checked back into their rooms a day early, and then again just after eight o'clock when the pair finished their dinner at the TroutHunter and asked their waitress if any bars had live music. He'd said he'd be right over in case there was trouble. Jan had relayed all that news to Steve and Lara.

As per Lara's plan, he signaled the men's arrival by singing "Bad Moon Rising." After much debate, and after he saw in her eyes how much she needed to help, not just wanted to help, he had reconsidered listening to her suggestions. He wanted to show that he trusted and needed her—he just hoped he wasn't making a mistake by agreeing to let Lara lead the detectives on a wild goose chase until the FBI arrived. Still, he truly didn't believe the bad guys would hurt her if they didn't have to. At least, not before she led them to him.

Of course, the last part of her plan, the part on the river, was madness. He just prayed she was right that this would avoid any desperate gunplay and make for easier collection of the criminals and their evidence.

When he started the song, Lara inched her way toward him, covering her movements by stopping to speak with several patrons. As the song neared its end, she leaned her crutches on a post, hopped to the mic and stood beside Steve.

The crowd clapped and whistled loudly. Steve slid his guitar strap over his head and then reached for Lara and gave her a big hug. The crowd hushed.

"I know you are all fans of Steve's by now," Lara called out, "and some of you know that we sing together sometimes."

The crowd clapped and whistled some more. Someone at the bar yelled, "Sing with him again now!"

She smiled. "We will sing together in the next set, but what I wanted you to know is that Steve and I have been friends since high school. We grew up as best friends in California, and I think you should join with me in telling Steve that we would love to have him stay in Island Park from here on out."

Steve grinned. Before she could say another word, he took Lara tightly in his arms and gave her a long, lingering kiss. The audience went wild. Then Steve walked casually out through the back door.

Behind him he heard Lara, her voice reasonably breathless, say into the microphone, "Steve will be back in five minutes with his last set for the night, so fill your glasses and settle in. Thank you."

* * *

Lara sat down at the end of the bar and glanced at the two men sitting in the back of the room; Steve had whispered to her when she hugged him about where they were sitting. People were quizzing her about Steve, but she just smiled and told them it was early in their relationship but she hoped it would progress.

Her hand shook as she lifted a shot of brandy to her mouth. She could feel the criminals' eyes upon her, but they were keeping their seats and hadn't moved. She was thankful for that.

Jan approached from the back. She had been designated to watch the two men, and she was also on the lookout for any other strangers they might have brought back with them. She set to wiping off the counter in front of Lara and whispered, "Steve's gone. Time for your song."

Lara took a deep breath and stepped onto the bar's tiny stage. The crowd immediately quieted, expecting her to make an important announcement. Instead she surprised everyone by picking up Steve's guitar and strumming it. Then, leaning into the mic, she said, "Steve asked me to start off this set, but you all should feel free to help out. 'All the leaves are brown…'"

The crowd stayed mostly quiet, though there were a few whistles and cheers as she began to sing. Her voice was shaky, and the crowd seemed to sense her uneasiness. Still, she found her center and they began to sing along as she got into the meat of "California Dreamin'".

McKay and Johnson stayed where they were, surprising Lara. Susan served them another round of beers, and by the second verse Johnson—Lara assumed, because he was half the size of the other man—joined in. Too soon, however, the song was over and the crowd was restlessly waiting for Steve.

Lara scanned the room, making a show of looking for Steve. When he didn't reappear, she held up her finger and walked toward the back door. Jan passed her, throwing her bar cloth over her shoulder and heading to the mic.

"Maybe that kiss was too much for Steve!" she called. The crowd laughed, and when the mirth died down Jan added, "Lara will go get him, though, so drink up. I'm sure he'll be right back."

Following the plan, Lara waited outside for a few minutes. Coming back in, she said to the audience, "I'm sorry, folks, but I can't seem to find Steve. I think I know where he is, though. While I go get him, we'll turn on some music for you to dance."

Lara noted McKay and Johnson out of the corner of her eye. The two threw some money on the table and went quickly out the front door. So, now was the time for her to get in her jeep and take these boys for a little ride.

It worked. She saw their black truck in her rearview mirror, hanging back as much as it could but still there as they made to tail her. She went at a snail's pace up the high winding mountain road she'd chosen, as it was the same dirt trail she and Steve had taken earlier and in the darkness the one lane was even more treacherous—and her cumbersome cast made driving extremely dangerous. At first it felt weird, driving with one leg in a cast, but she would manage anything when it came to saving her lover's life.

She kept McKay and Johnson weaving and swerving on the road to Sawtelle Peak for almost an hour. Her ankle ached to her butt. When she reached the summit, she got out and stood on crutches there, her back to the road. Then she waited for the crunching steps of the men and prayed they wouldn't assault her where she stood. They would have to be extremely foolhardy to do so.

They didn't. Their soft footsteps ceased, and Lara assumed they were watching from hiding. Knowing the men were only steps away, in her best imitation of Jennifer Lawrence she whispered into the thin night air, "Damn it, Steve, I thought for sure you would be up here. Where the hell are you? And what are you running from?"

She waited for ten minutes there, giving the men time to retreat to their vehicle. Then she slowly made her way back to her jeep and down the mountain.

They followed. It was almost one a.m. before she got back to her house, and the guys were still behind her, tailing at the farthest distance they could manage. She'd expected that, though. After planting the seed that she was indeed involved with Steve, they would stick to her like glue until she found him. She went inside and tried to get a little sleep, but after a couple of hours tossing and turning she gave up and sat in her loft, thinking.

At nine a.m., she walked to her jeep and headed to the clinic in West Yellowstone to get a new cast; she had to have a walking cast in order to put the next step of the plan into action. She'd made this appointment the day before, telling the nurse she'd ruined the one she had, and after convincing them of that fact she proceeded to annihilate the old one.

She saw the vehicle of the men outside her house. It followed her the thirty miles to West Yellowstone, Montana, and they were still there when she stepped out of the doctor's clinic sporting a new hot-pink walking cast. She lifted her chin upward and scowled at a dingy sky hanging so low that she thought if she lifted her hand she could touch it, then walked stiff-legged toward her jeep. The walking cast was cumbersome and slowed her progress, but it was much better than using the crutches.

The detectives followed her back to Island Park. She pretended to be talking on her phone all the way. When she reached The TroutHunter, she parked and went in. The men stayed outside in the big parking lot. She didn't know exactly where they were, but she could feel their binoculars boring into her.

Lawrence came out to help her hitch to a trailer where a canoe was tied. After, Lara took her seat behind the wheel of her jeep and adjusted the rearview mirror. Her own appearance startled her. Her skin held a grayish tint, much the color of today's sky. Her eyes were deep-set and scared. A shiver of apprehension coursed through her system, turning her blood to ice. If the last step to her plan and Steve's didn't work, this could be their last day together. *Their last day alive.*

Wanting to get the whole thing over with one way or another, Lara started the jeep and drove out onto Highway 20, heading south toward the Mesa Falls scenic drive. As she left the main road and headed east, the terrain changed abruptly. Sage prairies replaced the lodge poles in some sites, and the ground looked flat and wide. A strong afternoon wind rustled the trees and bent the tall grass and abundant wildflowers to the ground. As she drove further, there were cleared areas that had been logged of all trees and alternating stands of pines. The dark sky had begun spitting rain, and it didn't look like it had any intention of stopping.

The old highway was rutted and rough, making travel slower than Lara felt like driving. But she had the canoe on her hitch, and if she weren't careful she'd shake it right off. Frost heaves from heavy winters made some spots seem like a roller-coaster ride.

Lara cautiously adjusted her mirror and made sure the black truck was still about a quarter of a mile behind her. A wash of cold terror saturated her body, but this was what needed to happen. Her trepidation wouldn't leave until the day was over.

She watched for a wooden forest sign that read HATCHERY FORD ROAD 351, and then she made the turn. Her hands shook as she tried to steer the jeep with its heavy load. This new road made the one she'd turned off seem like a million dollar highway. The dirt lane was more like a cattle trail, and there were several forks along the way. Only locals and avid fisherman would know about this route. If her pursuers took one wrong turn, they could lose her for hours. She had to make sure that they stayed close now, so she watched carefully until she saw the black SUV following.

Lara shook her head at the irony. She wanted nothing better than to never see these jerks again, and yet, her future and Steve's depended on them staying close. She knew that this was exactly where they would have hidden their own canoe to head for their money. But they needed Steve dead to live out their dreams of grandeur.

The dirt road had grass growing up in the middle, and her trailer and deep puddles of muddy water slowed Lara's progress. On the sides here, the trees grew thick. Lara usually stopped several times while driving this road to examine the varieties of flowers. Today she just called out their names, trying to calm her frayed nerves.

"Evening primrose, sticky geranium, western columbine, Indian paintbrush, fireweed, clematis, lupine, goat's beard...." Her shaky voice only made things worse, so she turned her thoughts to her last hours with Steve, holding on desperately to the fact that he loved her. It helped.

The sound of her jeep startled a bald eagle from its perch high in a lodge pole pine. The bird flew ahead, following the road as if guiding her, and Lara took comfort in its huge wingspan and elegant movement. It was as if God had given her a sign, a guardian of sorts. That image consoled her for a few minutes as well.

She finally came to the next sign she'd been anticipating. It said FOUR-WHEEL VEHICLES ONLY, as the road became rocky and descended rapidly into a deep canyon. Lara could hear the rushing of the river, and passing a broken-down cabin, the chimney the only thing left standing, she wondered again, as she did every time she came down here, who had been lucky enough to once live in this beautiful and remote area.

Lara quickly drove the last few feet to the cement boat ramp that was her destination. Behind her, the black truck passed, the men obviously trying to act inconspicuous. Ahead, wide and gorgeous, the Henry's Fork River pushed its way eastward.

This particular location was the last place fishermen could get out of the river before it became too treacherous to continue, was the last stop before getting dangerously close to the falls. Lara usually picked up her clients here at the end of a trip and shuttled them back to her uncle's establishment. This time, Lara was getting into the river where she should be getting out.

This part of the plan had been hers. It was important her pursuers thought she was going to meet Steve so that they followed. She also needed time to get down the river a ways before they caught up.

She hoped this wasn't a mistake. She'd told Steve that she'd navigated this section of the river one other time, but she'd never been past the point of the danger signs before. She had studied the river above Mesa Falls on foot many times, though, and she was sure that if she paddled very hard, and if someone was near the edge of the falls with ropes, she could get to shore before going over the edge. That was the plan. She knew that in her condition this was risky, but she also knew Steve would never allow her to help if she didn't feel confident…and she just had to make sure he was okay or die trying. This was the only way to be sure he knew how sorry she was for hurting him in the past, as this was the ultimate apology.

She also knew that Steve would be waiting to pull her from the fast white water and begin the rest of their lives together.

Thunder rolled down the canyon along the river, sounding like a bowling ball headed toward the pins. The late afternoon rain had become a chill and miserable drizzle, and Lara worked as quickly as possible with numb fingers untying the cords and ropes on her canoe. The knowledge that the black truck loomed above on the mountaintop slowed her progress further, but she kept at it, shivering uncontrollably in her lightweight yellow slicker.

She finished with the cords. Backing the trailer up to the bank, Lara slid her canoe halfway into the river; then she got back into the jeep and moved it away from the ramp. Smiling weakly to herself, she slipped a life jacket over her raincoat. If she didn't get stopped before the one-hundred-and-fourteen-foot drop-off, a life jacket would do her absolutely no good.

A strong wind rose as Lara eased her canoe into the central flow of water. The wind would help her get to her destination faster, but it could also propel her too far, and as she rounded the second bend in this uncharted part of the river, a new danger reared its ugly head; she heard the detectives' truck roar to life and thunder down to the launch ramp.

The men would be on the river in a matter of minutes.

Lara paddled with every ounce of strength she possessed.

Chapter Twenty-Three

As suggested by Lara, Steve had spent Friday night hidden in the attic of the lodge at Mesa Falls. The charming structure had been erected as an inn in 1912, when the establishment was a stagecoach stop for tourists en route to Yellowstone National Park. Thick logs still held the building together in a remarkable stately fashion, and the main floor had been renovated into an interpretive center and gift shop.

Last night he had climbed to the second floor and torn a board off a window after the lodge closed for the evening, as Lara said the security was lax and they could repair any damage later. Now Steve went quietly down to the main floor, to a small room where displays of animals and their bones were displayed, and he casually walked into the main rooms where tourists mingled and read script under pictures, looked at displays and thumbed through books at the gift shop. No one took any notice.

He stepped out onto the wide veranda that framed the lodge. The skies were grey and it was drizzling, but he could hear the roar of the falls and a shiver went through him thinking of Lara. *Oh, dear God, please keep her safe.* She'd said no one ever lived who fell from the cliff into the boiling water below.

He checked the pistol he'd brought and hurried along the main trail toward the upper Mesa Falls, but as soon as he had a clear opening he left the groomed trail and climbed through the dense undergrowth toward a place where he had already left ropes and a few different supplies. Driggs would be waiting for him there; he'd supposedly flown into the area that morning with backup.

Driggs was indeed waiting, and he whispered to Steve that two other agents would appear at any moment. Steve nodded without speaking then looked around. The rocks of the path were slippery with green moss. He prayed that Lara's plan had gone the way she imagined, and that she would round the dangerous bend of the river close enough to catch his rope and be pulled to safety.

Leaving Driggs, he went down to the agreed-upon spot, and the resplendence of the falls there was rivaled only by their danger. Rock cliffs loomed on either side, making the area seem wildly primitive. The opposite side of the canyon was a sheer cliff covered in a brilliant green moss.

Steve's ropes had been secured, but looking down over the falls scared him to death. What if the current grew too strong for some reason? What if Lara couldn't grab the ropes? She'd seemed so sure this plan would work. She'd done it before, she'd said. God, he hoped she wasn't lying. And she couldn't have done it before with a cast! Why had he let her talk him into this?

The rain, which only moments earlier had been a fine drizzle, became a downpour, and the harsh clamor of the falls sent spasms of a sick dark fear through him. To make matters worse, a dense fog had crept in. He should have had a perfect view upstream for a quarter of a mile, but the misty cloud cover and rainy conditions blurred his vision. Enormous boulders stuck out of the river like great humpback whales. If Lara's canoe hit one of those, it would break apart.

Slipping on a raincoat and leather gloves, Steve looked up the river and then down. He absorbed the HAZARDOUS AREA signs with a growing dread, and then ran along the slick trail to see if he could spot her.

Nothing.

He returned to the agreed upon spot and stepped out onto the slippery rocks to make sure he had a strong foothold. The weather had made this much more dangerous than it had seemed last night when he'd hid the equipment; the rocks grew more treacherous with ever moment of pouring rain. He tested the ropes and their strength against the huge stones he'd tied them to, and was mostly satisfied.

The roar of the falls screamed in his ears from just fifty yards away, and he knew he couldn't count on yelling to Lara over the din of the raging water that descended with a one hundred and fourteen foot drop downward into the belly of the canyon; the sound of that water rushing over rock, combined with the wind and rain, made it almost impossible to hear anything else.

A sharp whistle sounded behind him, so Steve turned. Driggs and the two other FBI agents walked forward.

They all shook hands and introduced themselves.

"Everything ready up above?" Steve asked. He appreciated that Driggs had brought other men with him.

"Yep," Driggs said. "We're in position. The only way those bastards will get away is by going over the falls…and if they choose that route, we'll pick them up in a couple of days when their bodies wash up somewhere down below. Considering what they've done, that might be too good an end for them."

"Here she comes!" the agent named Brooks called out.

Steve looked away and saw Lara appear out of the mist, expertly dodging a rock five feet in diameter. He grabbed his rope and waded out into the icy water, moving as far as he could get without being pulled away by the current. Driggs and Brooks took positions and followed, each of them providing one more anchor point.

Now it was totally up to Lara.

* * *

Easing the nose of her canoe toward Steve, Lara paddled harder. She couldn't make out the features of his face, but she knew he was every bit as scared as she was. The final stretch of rapids was straight ahead. If she didn't reach him and his rope within the next few feet, she'd go over the falls.

"Here it comes, honey," Steve yelled over the din of the falls, pointing also. "Grab the rope!"

He threw, but as Lara lunged…her canoe hit a slightly submerged rock. She lost her balance and the craft capsized. The weight of her cast pulled her down, and Lara was dragged under the raging water.

Was this how she would die? Was she being punished for that mistake all those years ago? Was this her final proof of how stupid she'd been, how you could never earn back something you'd so carelessly flung away? Was this proof that forgiveness only came in the next life, and she'd have to hope to meet Steve then?

No. That was foolish. She just had to work harder.

She had to get her head up. The water wasn't extremely deep, but it was treacherously swift. The life jacket helped, and when her face pushed through the surface, she saw the rope floating in front of her.

"Lara!"

Steve's muffled screams spurred her to action, and in the next split second she gripped the lifeline and was pulled to safety. As she was, she fancied she heard the faint crash of her canoe hitting the rocks below the falls.

Three men looked down at her. Steve shouted, "My God, are you all right?"

Lara nodded, but she couldn't answer. Trying to breathe took all of her effort.

Two men introducing themselves as Brooks and Driggs quickly carried her onto a flat surface out of harm's way.

"Get ready, Steve," Driggs urged. "McKay and Johnson could be here at any minute. They did follow you, didn't they?" he asked, turning back to Lara.

"I...I think so. I didn't see them get into the water, but they drove down to the ramp. There were canoes for them to use, too. There was another one hidden in the bushes, maybe the one they used to stash the money in the first place."

Driggs turned away, looking satisfied, and Lara breathed a sigh of exhausted relief. She had done her part. Now the rest was up to the FBI.

And Steve.

* * *

McKay and Johnson had indeed followed. Steve barely had time to get back in the water before another boat appeared from the mist, and apparently the noise of the falls scared one of the detectives because frantic shouting was heard above the chaos of the rushing water.

Johnson acted as if he'd had little experience at rowing, and from Steve's position it looked like the two detectives were working against each other. The heavy canoe suddenly spun and hit a rock broadside. For a minute Steve wondered if either could make it to safety. They weren't wearing life jackets.

Steve didn't want them dead. That would be too easy. He wanted them alive and ready to pay for the hell they'd put him and Lara through, for the crimes they'd committed against numerous victims. He did have to admit, however, that he was also grateful to them in a strange way. Without their actions he might never have found Lara again.

Their canoe suddenly bumped another rock and turned. This time it was headed straight for Steve and the agents, and the two detectives saw them. The pair started paddling together, but that only made things worse. The front of their canoe wedged between two boulders.

"Hey, you guys!" McKay yelled. "Help us, goddamnit!"

Steve waded out and jumped on one of the rocks. A moment later he had his pistol aimed directly at McKay's head. "Give me your gun."

"Mitchell," the man gasped. "You son of a bitch."

Steve heard two more guns unholstered behind him. "Listen to me, McKay," he said. "You can give me your weapons, take this rope and save your damn necks then get what's coming to you, or you can take your chances with the falls. It's a quite a drop, but nobody knows how deep the water is. I don't know of anyone going over those falls who's lived, but I guess there's always a first time…."

There was no hesitation from Johnson. He handed Steve a weapon, handle first.

"Good," Steve said. "Maybe you'll be smart enough to make a deal when you see the evidence we have on you—and on your friend."

Johnson looked back at McKay and then shrugged. Steve grinned and watched him get pulled to shore. A moment later the man was led up the trail with two guns at the back of his head.

McKay glared at Steve and Steve's gun, all the while cussing. Finally he handed over his pistol and said, "Throw me a rope, you dirty bastard."

Steve got him back to shore with little problem. There he handcuffed McKay and followed the others, but a twist of fate got the better of him. A slick rock had escaped his notice, and his foot hit it heavily and he lost his balance. The lurch was for only a split second, but that's all McKay needed. He twisted free of Steve's grip, scooted his cumbersome body around a rotting tree trunk and was off into the mist.

There was no time to call for backup. Swearing softly, Steve knew he would have to go after him alone.

Thunder crashed as he headed into the darkened forest.

* * *

Would this nightmare ever end? The racket of the forceful water from the falls was driving Lara crazy, and now Steve had left the marked trail in pursuit of a dangerous man on a perilous mountain. She stood frozen in amazed horror as she watched McKay slip away.

"Steve!" she yelled above the cacophony. "Forget him! He's handcuffed and he doesn't have a gun. It's slippery on the cliffs. Don't go after him!"

Her cries were surely absorbed by the raging torrents below.

* * *

After giving chase through dense underbrush for several hundred sloped yards, Steve realized the danger was too great. The steep canyon in the dark of a thunderstorm was an impossible hike. No fit man could accomplish it, not to mention a fat, unhealthy one in handcuffs. He wouldn't go after McKay. He'd let Driggs and Brooks take it from here. He had too much to live for.

Turning, he headed back toward the secure path, but he caught sight of a light windbreaker just below him on the cliff. It was McKay, who stood precariously close to the rim of the gorge, the water boiling beneath him. He must have slipped and ended on a lower outcropping.

"McKay," he yelled.

"Come and get me, Mitchell!"

"I'm not that stupid! It's your choice, McKay. No one can save you this time but yourself."

McKay looked over his shoulder at the far side of the river where Steve guessed he'd hidden his loot; then he looked back at Steve. "Not without my money."

"That's your choice," Steve called. "We can go get it." The loot was what he'd been looking for all along.

McKay looked down once again at the white turbulence below, and Steve wondered what he was thinking.

"Give me a hand, Mitchell. It's slick as hell here."

Steve hesitated, wondering if the man would try anything underhanded. At last he decided it was his job to help if at all possible, so he braced himself and then took a step closer, bending down and reaching out his arm.

McKay had to shift his body to reach above him to where Steve perched. The man did so…and then Steve felt McKay make one last grab, obviously trying to pull him off balance. It was a foolhardy attempt, and with a sickening swiftness McKay slipped backwards. His hands clawed the slimy moss for an instant, and then he was gone from sight. His screams of terror were quickly swallowed up by the sounds of the churning mass of water below.

Chapter Twenty-Four

Lara was once again resting comfortably in bed, her pink cast nestled in a stack of pillows, when Steve called up from the kitchen.

"That was Driggs on the phone. He said we owe him a fishing trip when your leg is healed. Also…they found the money. They had reinforcements from the forest service help them retrieve it. It wasn't even buried or hidden! It was sitting behind a big boulder, in plain sight just like Lawrence said it would be. Johnson's in for a long time, even if he only did what McKay told him. More importantly, babe, this is finally over."

Lara could hear the relief in his voice, and his happiness was almost tangible. She felt the same. Nothing seemed impossible now. Dreams really did come true.

She could hear Steve puttering around fixing breakfast. Lawrence and Jan had insisted that both of them take a couple of days off to recuperate after their ordeal, and neither of them protested. Lara felt like she could sleep for a week.

"Lara," Steve called again, this time with the excitement of a little boy. "I'm going to call my parents! I haven't been able to speak to them for months. My dad loves to fish. Could we invite them up?"

She could deny him nothing. Even if she could have, she had no wish to. "I'd love that."

Steve's parents. How long since she'd seen them, and how wonderful it would be to show that she'd changed. To show that she and Steve were going to have the life he'd always deserved. The life that *they'd* always deserved. It was only a matter of reaching out and taking it.

Steve carried a tray of pastries and coffee up the stairs.

"You keep feeding me like this, and I'll be as fat as a toad by the time I get the cast off," Lara complained with a grin, taking a bite of a cinnamon bun.

"I plan on getting you fat, my love—but not this way."

Lara felt food catch in her throat. This was a very serious subject for her. It had been in the back of her mind for years, and thinking about it still caused her tremendous anguish. What was Steve thinking? She couldn't have children. She'd told him as much that night she told him about Phillip.

"What are you saying, Steve?" Her voice trembled as she asked.

Steve set down his coffee mug and cupped her chin. "I'm saying that I want to have a child with you. It doesn't matter to me how we have her, really. We can try for a while normally, and that'll be tons of fun." He grinned and kissed the top of her nose. "If it doesn't work, we'll consider other options. My only requirement is that her last name be Mitchell. So...will you take my name, Lara? I want to marry you."

Lara felt the last band of despair spring from her heart, a band she hadn't even realized remained. Steve's request had freed her from any fear that they might not be perfectly matched.

"Yes," she told him, taking his face in her hands. "I would *love* to be your wife. I never thought I'd get another chance."

She kissed him with silent promises of beautiful future together then asked, "What about your job?"

Steve shook his head, and she noticed quiet conviction in his eyes. "I'm through with that, Lara. I'm burned out, like I said that night on the mountain. I made up my mind even before I found you again."

Lara just watched him, waiting to hear what he would say next. She would go with him wherever he needed to be.

"I've built my life in the city. You have to be rugged in a different way there, and it made me a sour person." He shook his head. "I'm not knocking that lifestyle, it's just that...well, while I was in the mountains I learned a lot about myself. Out *there* is what mankind has made, but here is where we can get back to reality. The land itself changed me somehow. The day I stepped from the tangled forest and looked down on Island Park, I felt like I was coming home."

"Yes?" Lara prompted.

"Those weeks in the Yellowstone backcountry helped decide me. When you live in a place like this you begin to realize how important things are that we usually take for granted: warm sunlight, a peaceful night's sleep, pure unconditional love, those kinds of things. You know, Lara, you and Island Park brought me back to reality. I finally came to terms with who I am. Better yet, I found the music again. I'm going to start writing."

Lara bubbled with excitement. "Will you still sing in the Buffalo Room?"

Steve grinned. "Of course. I've got some ideas for specific music I want to write, and the bar is a great place to try out new compositions. And my life with you is the most important thing."

"For me too," Lara whispered. "Forever."

Steve hugged her tight. "If we want it bad enough, we can do anything. I can do anything as long as you're in it with me." He took Lara's hand and raised it to his lips. "This place is really amazing. It cured our past and it saved my future."

Lara sighed. "A friend and client once said the same thing to me. This place is magical. Its power is boundless."

She rose and took Steve by the hand, leading him up onto the upper deck and into a cloudless morning. There she admitted, "The only thing I love more than this place is the people: Jan, my uncle…and most of all you, Steve. You came here and you gave me another chance, and you got another chance of your own. I never thought it could work out so perfectly. I love you."

Looking in the same direction, Steve and Lara began their new life together with a start at inner peace, impossibly beautiful surroundings and the promise of friends and family—and with a kiss.

The End

ABOUT THE AUTHOR

Lyn Austin is a popular and award-winning author. Her novels *The Quiet Storm*, *The Auction*, and her short story "Carol of the Heart" received excellent reviews. Lyn has been a guest speaker throughout the United States, as well as in many other countries. Her non-fiction works *Sisters of the Sole* and *Prism of Light* can be found at Smashwords.

Visit Lyn at www.romancenovelsbylyn.com.

Did you enjoy this book? Drop us a line and say so! We love to hear from readers, and so do our authors. To connect, visit www.boroughspublishinggroup.com online, send comments directly to info@boroughspublishinggroup.com, or friend us on Facebook and Twitter. And be sure to check back regularly for contests and new releases in your favorite subgenres of romance!

Are you an aspiring writer? Check out www.boroughspublishinggroup.com/submit and see if we can help you make your dreams come true.

www.ingramcontent.com/pod-product-compliance
Lightning Source LLC
Chambersburg PA
CBHW060821120626
46557CB00001B/313